The Fall

By
Robin Alexander

THE FALL
© 2014 BY ROBIN ALEXANDER

All rights reserved. No part of this book may be reproduced in printed or electronic form without permission. Please do not participate in or encourage piracy of copyrighted materials in violation of the author's rights. Purchase only authorized editions.

ISBN 13: 978-1-935216-66-7

First Printing: 2014

This trade paperback is published by
Intaglio Publications
Walker, LA USA
WWW.INTAGLIOPUB.COM

This is a work of fiction. Names, characters, places, and incidents are the product of the author's imagination or are used fictitiously, and any resemblance to actual persons, living or dead, businesses, companies, events, or locales is entirely coincidental.

CREDITS

EXECUTIVE EDITOR: TARA YOUNG
COVER DESIGN BY: Tiger Graphics

Dedication

For Ruth and Laura, who have been falling for thirty-two years. Now they can finally legally put a ring on it. Congratulations and love to you both!

Acknowledgments

Tara, I have no idea what I'd do without you. I pray I never find out.

Chapter 1

"Okay, listen up. We have one giant-ass badger to paint, and I don't wanna be here all night. I want two on the head, two on the jersey, and two on the lettering. Coach Perkins has promised to make us run until we puke if we get paint on the gym floor. The colors are already premixed and numbered. If you look at the diagram I gave you, you'll see that the numbers correspond with the area you're working on. That's right, people, it's paint by number. So y'all decide what part you want and get to it."

Harper Guidry frowned as her six-person crew began to bicker over colors and badger body parts. Twenty people had volunteered, and had they all shown up, the project would've been finished in an hour. As it stood, she'd be there half the night with a group of dorks, one of whom stuck his tongue in the paint to the cheers of his buddies. Harper was seriously regretting her appointment of project leader.

Across the gym peeking out from behind the stands, another girl watched the group nervously as she contemplated making her move. Lydia Chase didn't know Harper, but she hoped that would change very soon. Between classes, she walked a few feet behind Harper unnoticed, gazing at shiny long hair and admiring a shapely backside. Harper had curves the twigs who starved themselves couldn't compete with. Lydia had grown tired of skulking around hoping that Harper would set her green-eyed gaze on her. She was about to force the hand of fate and hoped it didn't bitch-slap her for the trouble.

"Lydia Chase, reporting for duty under protest."

Harper turned and found a girl standing erect, her hand held to her head in salute. Both wrists were covered in corded bracelets that went halfway up her arms. Though it was only the first week of October, she was wearing a knit cap; wisps of bright blond hair stuck out from beneath it. Both of her ears were full of studs, including the cartilage. Gray blue eyes regarded Harper with disdain.

"I don't remember meeting you when you signed up," Harper said, trying to recall Lydia's face.

"I didn't sign up for this bullshit. I'm here to serve out a sentence. Mrs. Talbot gave me the choice between doing this and detention."

Harper frowned. "Do you even know how to paint?"

"Let's see." Lydia put her hands on her hips and looked up at the ceiling. "You stick a brush into a bottle, then rub it on paper while staying inside the lines. I'm not on the honor roll, but I think I can handle it."

Harper wasn't thrilled with the bohemian brat's attitude, but she was stuck with her. "You can paint the pants with me. We'll be using the red in those bottles over there. Grab a brush."

The rest of her crew had finished bickering and was settling into the project. Harper sighed, picked up a brush, and knelt down near where Lydia was preparing to begin working. "What'd you get detention for?"

"I didn't know Talbot was behind me, and I called Scooter Nixon a dick."

"He is a dick," Harper said with a chuckle.

Lydia got down on her stomach, her feet in the air as she began to paint the badger's pants in the crotch. "I know Louisiana isn't a liberal state, but I'd hoped that it would be a little more up with the times than Arkansas, but nope. It's 2013, for Pete's sake. And what sucks badger dick is having to wear a uniform to a public school."

"You're right, that does blow, but at least we're talking khaki pants and polos here. At least we're not stuck with plaid skirts and starched shirts. And hey, we're not all narrow-minded pinheads."

"Scooter is," Lydia said with a derisive laugh. "And all of his friends. I truly don't understand the groupies who kiss his ass hoping that he'll be their bud, so they can be popular. I'd rather shove nails up my butthole." She stopped painting for a second and stared at Harper. "Do you hang with his crowd?"

"I would if I only had half a brain. Even if they aren't stupid, most of the jocks here pretend to be because they think they're being cool. Do you know Mason Savino?"

"I don't, but I know who he is." Lydia resumed painting. "Is that your boyfriend?"

"My cousin, and he's been on the honor roll since first grade, but you'd never know that by talking to him. He dumbs down to fit in. He's sweet, though, and if Scooter is blowing you shit, I can tell Mason to make him back off."

"I can handle myself, thanks. That makes Corey Savino your cousin, too, then."

"Yeah, so don't confuse me with one of her groupies," Harper said with a sigh.

"What're we painting this for?"

"The football team is gonna run through it at the start of the homecoming game." Harper held up both hands defensively. "I know it's cliché and stupid, it wasn't my idea. Coach Perkins wants to go retro, and he asked the art department to make this. I got stuck with being in charge of it."

Lydia grinned devilishly. "Can I paint a rainbow flag on his belt buckle?"

"No."

"Why—because that would offend you?"

"Not at all. This is the version of the mascot they had when Coach Perkins went to school here. He wants it to be exactly as it was then. I'm not homophobic if that's what you're thinking. My aunt is gay."

Lydia's brow rose. "She single?"

"She's too old for you."

"Shit." Lydia went back to painting. "There's half a dozen lesbians at this school, and they're all couples. So…how old is your aunt?"

Harper laughed. "She's thirty-five, and you're jailbait."

"My mom's gay, single, and almost as hot as I am."

"Your humility amazes me," Harper said with a smile.

Lydia nodded. "Okay, I've decided that you may be kind of cool, so please don't do anything to ruin that," she said with bravado, but she was jelly on the inside as she gazed at the dimples on Harper's cheeks, her fair skin, and the tiny cleft in her chin.

"Can I call you Bo? That's short for bohemian, which is the word that comes to mind when I look at you."

"And just like that, you're ruining my opinion of you. Give someone an inch, and they take a mile."

Harper laughed. "So you moved here from Arkansas. What part?"

"Little Rock, only slightly less boring than Baton Rouge, but it does seem to have a tiny LGBT community."

"You don't sound like you're from Arkansas. Your accent sounds more Northern." Harper watched Lydia pull the knit cap from her head and toss it aside. Her messy short blond hair stood on end with the help of static electricity caused by the hat.

Lydia nodded as she concentrated on her painting. "Midwest, I was born in Missouri, but we didn't live there very long. I get it from my mom, but I think she's starting to sound more Southern."

"How long have you been here?"

"We moved a month before school started."

"So…just to be totally clear, you are a lesbian, right?"

Lydia met Harper's gaze. "I am, and I'm damn proud of it."

"That's pretty cool."

"Glad you think so," Lydia said with a smirk. "I'd hate to get another detention for painting you and this ugly-ass badger."

Noel Savino leapt off her porch and released a happy sigh as the first real autumn wind sent her hair flying and blew leaves out of the trees. The weather seemed to cool as soon as October arrived and had mercifully stayed that way after a blistering summer. Fall was her favorite time of year, and as she passed one of the two houses between her and her parents' place, she was thrilled to see that the Sutters had already lined the walk in front of their home with pumpkins and mums.

The breeze brought something else delightful to Noel's attention—the aroma of her mother's spaghetti sauce. Inez cooked the same meal every Friday night, she served leftovers on Saturday and roast on Sundays. The elder Savinos' home was the hub of all family activity.

"The baby's here, now we can eat," Joe Savino announced when Noel walked in the front door.

"We eat when I say we eat," Inez yelled from the kitchen.

Joe's hair was inky black from a recent dye job and combed into a pompadour. Even though his children teased him about the old style, Joe preferred it because he felt it gave him a gangster look, and Inez liked that. His so-called tough image was marred by his wardrobe, which normally consisted of long basketball shorts and a short-sleeved button-down shirt.

Parked in his recliner in front of the TV, Joe threw up his hands. "She kills me. I ask when we can eat, and she says when you get here. Now you're here, and we wait."

It amused Noel that even though her parents had lived in Louisiana for almost forty-seven years, they still retained their Long Island accents. Noel and her siblings spoke a mixture of Southern drawl and a New York Italian accent. She smiled and kissed her father's cheek. "You fish today?"

Joe scowled. "Me and Jeff, we call it 'taking the boat out' when we don't catch nothin'. We took the boat out all day, and we're probably gonna do it again tomorrow."

Noel's brother, Matthew, walked into the living room and gave her a playful shove. "It's about time you got here. We're starving."

"You'll live." Noel patted the paunch on his stomach on her way to the kitchen. She stopped in the den where Harper was seated in front of her laptop. "What're you doing?" she asked with a smile.

Harper brushed a long dark lock of hair from her face and gazed up at Noel. "Homework."

"On a Friday?"

"I didn't have a chance to do it last night because I was painting the stupid badger, and I don't want it hanging over my head all weekend. You going to the game tonight?"

Noel held a finger to her lips and shook her head. She and Harper were the only two in the family who didn't particularly care about football. When Noel came out, they took it with a grain of salt, but had she admitted that she didn't adore the passing of the pigskin, she would've found herself pitched to the curb. So she and Harper pretended to be enamored with the Badgers, LSU, and the Saints football teams.

"You have to go, the whole family is going," Harper whispered.

"Homecoming games are too crowded, and I hate all the pomp and circumstance. If Dad gives me shit about not going, I'm depending on you to shove me down the steps or 'accidently' stab me."

"I do feel a sore throat coming on, the night air probably won't be good for me." Harper poked Noel in the arm. "You're the doctor, back me up on that."

"Dinner's on the table! Get in here!" Inez barked.

"Where's Lauren?" Noel asked when they all filed into the dining room.

"She's at the school with the kids doing her cheer mom thing," Matthew explained as he pulled Noel's chair out. He then did the same thing for Harper and bowed low. "For you, my lovely lady."

Inez stood next to her own chair looking at Joe expectantly, but her husband missed the subtle cue and sat down. Matthew raced over, pulled the chair out, and took his mother's hand as she sat. "You're a fine man, Matt, your mother raised you right, unlike your father, who was brought up by wolves."

"Sorry, I forgot." Joe put his hand to his chest. "You know I love you, kitten."

"Yeah, back at ya, Fido." Inez waved a hand. "Say the blessing."

"Wait, let me seat my big sister." Matthew pulled out Mary's chair, then quickly took his own. Joe waited until all heads were bowed and began his prayer. "Dear Lord, we thank you for this food. I'm a little disappointed that you didn't come through with the fish today, but I'm sure you had your reasons. I'm not sure what your plans are with the New Orleans Saints this Sunday, but if I may ask—"

Inez cleared her throat.

"Thank you for the food, Lord. Amen," Joe concluded and smiled. "Now we eat."

"Not yet, join hands," Inez said as she clasped Mary's hand and held the other out to Noel. "Y'all always forget the most important part."

"Kitten, can we do the family oath thing after dessert? I'm starving here," Joe complained.

Inez ignored him. "At this table, we are all equal. No one here is less, difference is a blessing. We love and support each other, and we'll do the same as our family grows bigger. The whole world can fall apart around us, but we will always stand together because we are the Savinos."

"So be it, let's eat," Joe said when everyone hoisted their glasses in agreement.

At four-foot-eleven and less than a hundred pounds, Inez was the leader of the Savino pack. With every passing year, she seemed to grow shorter, but she tried to compensate by teasing her hair to stand higher. To Noel, the youngest, she passed her bright green eyes; to Mary, her height and eye color, as well; and unfortunately to Matthew, the baldness that ran in the men on her side of the family.

Noel gazed at Mary as she poured dressing on her salad and admired the lone silver streak of hair that framed her face. "I like your hair that way, I'm glad you're not dyeing it anymore."

"You do?" Mary asked as she touched it. "I had to get it done so often that it was beginning to cost a fortune."

"I do your father's for less than ten bucks. Fancy salons are a waste of time and money," Inez said as she motioned for the pasta.

"And he looks like an old Elvis wannabe. You should stay outta the man's hair, Ma." Matthew chuckled when Joe playfully slapped the top of his shiny head.

"Matthew, do me a favor and go next door after dinner. Greg's gone on another sojourn, as he calls it, to find himself, and I promised we'd switch on a few lights each night. Do that for me," Inez said as she passed the salad to Noel.

"Where did he go this time?" Matthew asked.

Inez rolled her eyes. "Some retreat in the woods. I don't get it, he's the same person in his house, he isn't gonna be someone else out in the wilderness. I think it's an excuse to meet women, and what he's gonna find out there is a Bigfoot."

Matthew smiled at Mary. "Why don't you go out with the guy? He looks at you with stars in his eyes."

"I'm not interested in him that way. I don't know how many times I have to say that."

Inez shook her head. "I don't want my Mary with Greg. He's nice, but he's strange. He arranges his clothes in his closet according to color. Everyone knows shirts go with shirts and pants with pants. He does the same thing with his underwear and socks."

Noel's brow shot skyward. "How do you know this?"

"I looked. He's got girlie magazines in his bed stand, too."

"Momma, you can't dig through his things," Mary said incredulously.

"What kind of girlie magazines?" Joe shrugged when all the women at the table looked at him disapprovingly. "I was just curious."

"He's too neat for a man," Inez went on. "He's got everything arranged just so, and he owes the IRS. He's on a payment plan with them for back taxes."

"Momma!" Noel exclaimed.

"What? He gave me a key."

"You have one to my house, too. Do you go through my things when I'm not home?" Noel asked.

Inez stared at her for a moment, then said, "Joe, pour the wine, what're you waiting for?"

"Can I have some?" Harper asked.

Mary laughed. "Good try, baby girl."

"Let the girl have some vino. She's almost eighteen, for Pete's sakes," Joe argued.

"When she's eighteen, we'll talk." Mary waved her fork at her father and daughter. "No wine."

Noel was still disconcerted. "Momma, you dig through my things?"

"Why are you so worried? You got something to hide?"

"She's probably got girlie magazines, too," Matthew said with a laugh.

"I don't need those, I get plenty of the real thing. Probably more than you when you were single," Noel shot back with a wink.

"Are you seeing that girl you went to school with?" Inez asked.

Noel shook her head as she accepted a glass of wine from her father. "No, she just hangs out at my place every now and then. We do some girl bonding and bitching when she and her partner tie into it."

Inez wagged her finger at Noel. "You've been bonding with a lot of women since Brenna moved out, you're like denture cream. You're gonna get something if you don't behave."

"Please, do we have to discuss this at the dinner table?" Mary asked. "Harper doesn't need to hear this kind of talk."

"Yeah, I'm totally unaware that people have sex and sometimes contract STDs," Harper said with a sigh. "Again, I'm almost eighteen."

Inez spooned a huge helping of pasta onto Matthew's plate and motioned for Noel's. "Go light this time, please," Noel said as she passed it over.

Inez ignored her and piled the plate high. "That's your problem, you don't eat. A body needs food."

Noel threw up her hands. "I eat. Do I look emaciated to you?"

"You got no curves, a woman should have a shape, even lesbians." Inez frowned at Noel. "If you get lucky and find a full-bodied Italian woman, she'll snap you like a twig. Give her something to hold on to."

"I'm not eating all of that." Noel took the plate and raked some of the pasta onto Harper's.

"Ruth Noel Savino! You eat what I give you."

"Kitten, leave the girl alone. If she says she can't eat it all, she can't," Joe said.

Inez glared at him. "You know nothing about a woman's body, so hush."

"I know it takes up most of the bed, and it has a yap that's always open!"

"And hands that cook your food, clean your clothes, and take care of you when you're sick!" Inez countered hotly.

No one said a word as the two elders stared at each other. Joe finally shrugged. "You're right. I love you, kitten."

Inez waved a hand. "Back at you, Fido."

"I'll always butter your bread," Joe said as he pulled a slice from the basket.

Noel, Mary, and Matthew tensed, hoping the comment wouldn't prompt the retelling of the age-old bread story usually reserved for Sunday dinners. Mary tried to spare them all by saying, "I hope the Badgers win tonight. It's always sad when a team loses their homecoming game."

"It was a beautiful fall day just like this one in Long Island when your father first buttered my bread," Inez began, sounding like she was channeling Sophia Petrillo from the show *The Golden Girls*.

Matthew coughed to cover a groan.

"My brother Tony took me to a café to meet one of his friends, hoping that we'd fall in love and marry. The guy was a schmuck. He didn't even pull my chair out, then he talked to Tony more than he did me. I sat there listening to his blabbing when my eyes fell upon the most beautiful head of black hair. The man was an Adonis, and when he got up and left, that's when I noticed your father. He sat there with a sly grin, a pack of cigarettes rolled up in the sleeve of his T-shirt. I tried to play coy and picked up a slice of bread. Suddenly, he was at our table, he held out a gift, and—"

"And I said, 'A lady should never have to butter her own bread.'" Joe laughed. "I knew I had her then because she swooned."

"I was ducking because Tony started swinging." Inez smiled. "But I was impressed by how well you took a hit, that's why I slipped you my number when we got thrown outta that place."

Joe set the slice of bread onto a saucer and handed it to Matthew. "Pass that to your mother."

Inez smiled, kissed her fingertips, and held them to her heart. "He's been buttering my bread ever since."

There was a round of awws, then Harper set her fork aside. "Wow, my throat is really getting sore, I don't think I can finish my dinner."

Joe shook his head slowly. "Shoulda let her have that wine, Mary. The alcohol kills stuff."

"Yeah, like brain cells." Mary shot her father a look and set her gaze on Harper. "Do you feel bad?"

Harper nodded. "A little achy. I'm sorry, y'all, I don't think I can go to the game tonight."

Inez nudged Noel. "Check her for fever."

Noel went through the show of putting her hand on Harper's forehead and cheek. Harper gazed back at her with big green beseeching eyes. "She feels a little warm. Maybe she should stay home," Noel said and patted Harper's face. "I'm so sorry, Harpy. I know how much you were looking forward to going to the game. I'll stay with you."

Inez threw up a hand. "I'm not going, either."

"Noel's going to be with her," Mary said.

"What's Noel gonna do—check her teeth? She needs her nana to make her a special toddy. I'm staying home, and that's the end of it."

"I know sick, and you ain't sick," Inez said as soon as the others had left.

"I'm just worn down, Nana. I stayed at school late last night working on the poster, and I'm pooped," Harper said as she helped Noel clean the kitchen.

Inez shooed her away from the sink. "Then let me do this. Go home, take a hot bath, and go to bed."

Noel coughed. "I think I'm sick, too, Momma."

"You hush and wash the pots."

Harper wasted no time doling out kisses and took off to the garage apartment behind the house, her path illuminated by a security light. Noel and Inez watched her through the window above the kitchen sink. "That's my heart right there," Noel said with a laugh. "It was so nice of Mary to have a kid for me."

"She's a lot like you, that's for sure—stubborn and sneaky. Your sister has her hands full with that one, but she's a good kid." Inez sucked her teeth. "Mason and Corey, they give me and your brother a heart attack. Mason with his stupid pranks and Corey with her whoring around. Speaking of whoring—"

"Don't you start," Noel said. "You're making the whole family believe I'm a slut just because I'm not in a relationship."

"At your age, you should be."

"Mary's single, and you're not harping on her."

Inez dried a pan and put it away. "Mary doesn't have a string of men coming and going outta her apartment."

"Neither do I."

"Don't play coy. Every time I see you with a woman, it's someone I don't recognize. You're thirty-six, too old for that kinda playing around."

"Momma, I'm thirty-five."

"Whatever, you heard me. Knock it off."

Chapter 2

Bleary-eyed, Lydia pushed a grocery cart behind her mother. "Why do we have to do this at the butt crack of dawn on a Saturday, and why did I have to come with you?"

Sunny Chase held up a finger as she read the label on a can, then tossed it into the cart. "It's much less crowded, and I wanted you to come with me because I haven't seen you much this week." Sunny pursed her lips and grabbed a bag of rice. "I've never understood the difference between long and short grain."

Lydia consulted the list. "Uncle Ethan wants brown."

"Yuck, what's next?"

"Fennel. Do I even want to know what that is?"

Sunny made a face. "It's a weed that tastes like black jellybeans, it's horrid."

"Uncle Ethan needs to start driving again, so he can do this."

"He asks so little of us, shopping isn't a big deal," Sunny said distractedly as she pulled a box from the shelf and read the ingredients. "Besides, he spoils you rotten."

"Yeah, he's the grandmother I never had, dresses and all. I'm not complaining, I just wish he could drive. The last time I took him to a doctor's appointment, he screamed at me the whole way. And he freaked out when a squirrel ran out in front of us and said it could've flown through the windshield and killed him. A squirrel!" Lydia followed her mother as she moved farther down the aisle. "Are we really going to stay in Baton Rouge?"

Sunny tossed her favorite snack—a box of macaroni and cheese—into the cart. "I was promised that this would be my last transfer." She held up a hand when Lydia opened her mouth. "I know, we've heard that before, but this time if they don't stick to their word, I'm done. We have a great house, and you're happy with your school. You are happy, right?"

Lydia shrugged. "I'd be happier in a place where they had more LGBT students, but this is okay, and it's my last year," she said as she followed Sunny to the produce section. "Did I dream it last night, or were you and Ethan in my room again?"

Sunny smiled as she picked through the tomatoes. "I always peek in on you when you sleep. I've done it since you were a baby."

"That's just weird."

"Normally, you're a deep sleeper and don't notice."

"I thought I was dreaming when I heard Uncle Ethan talking to me like he does the cat. 'Oh, my sweet baby, so cute, so adorable, I could cry.' At least he didn't pet me."

"Actually, he was talking to Tobi. She sneaked into your room when we did."

Sunny hefted an armload of bags out of her Jeep and headed toward the back door. It swung open, and the sight that met her made her stagger. "How many times have I asked you to warn me when you're gonna go all kabuki?"

"Do I need to send out a memo before I give myself a facial?" Ethan tightened the belt on his red silk robe. "I don't know why it scares you. Who else is going to be in here with their face smeared with paste?"

"Oh, facial day, will there be primal screaming and waxing later?" Lydia followed Sunny inside and dropped the groceries onto the counter.

Ethan rifled through the bags that held produce. "I don't see the fennel."

"They didn't have any," Sunny said as Lydia went back out to get the rest of the food.

"Damn! There goes tomorrow night's recipe."

Sunny smiled and mouthed, *yes*, as she put a box of cereal into the pantry.

Ethan patted a cantaloupe. "Oh, just look at how perfect you are. I could just spank your little bottom. I hope you're sweet inside, unlike your rank cousin we couldn't eat last week."

"Fruit needs a lot of things to be sweet," Sunny said as she emptied another bag. "The right soil, sun, water, and affirmation from a tiny gay man wearing the guts of a cucumber on his face."

Ethan glared at her. His big blue eyes stood out against the pale yellow mask, and there was a cucumber seed on his nose. His curly gray hair was pulled away from his face and held by a thick pink band. The robe that would've been thigh length on a man of average height nearly dragged the floor.

"I've been giving myself facials since I was in my twenties. That's why now in my sixties, I don't have lines around my mouth that make it look like a butthole. If you don't start doing more for your skin, you're gonna have anus lips."

"Whoa," Lydia said as she walked in the door with the last of the groceries. "Part of me wishes I could've heard that whole conversation, and another part is so thankful that I didn't. I'm gonna go to my room and set up booby traps to alert me when y'all sneak in at night."

Ethan looked confused as Lydia walked out.

"We were busted last night. She's sleeping lighter these days."

"Ah," Ethan replied with a nod. He picked up a new bag of cat treats and shook it. A few seconds later, a gray and white cat darted into the kitchen yowling and looking at Ethan expectantly. "How's my little sport cat?" he cooed as he fed her one of the morsels. "Look how lithe and muscular you are. My girl has pretty eyes, yes, she does. Sunny, I want you to look at how white her whites are. Her chest, paws, and muzzle are just dazzling. There must be something in cat spit that's like bleach."

"Let's put her in the wash with the towels and see what happens."

Ethan shook his head with a disdainful look. "That kind of talk is why she uses your leg for a scratching post. She understands everything you say. Cats are brilliant, you know."

"If she's so smart, then why did she use my shoe as a litter box?"

Ethan looked as though the answer were obvious. "She hates you. If you spoke more kindly, she'd be nice."

Sunny stared at the cat. "Your whites are really pretty," she deadpanned.

Tobi shot her a "kiss my furry ass" look and sauntered off. Ethan grinned. "She sensed your insincerity," he said as he moved to the counter and began to dig into the bags again. "Later, I want to give you a facial. Your brows and upper lip need attention."

"I do not have a mustache!"

"Honey, you need a new light in your bathroom."

Before a car accident left Ethan blind in one eye and with slight paralysis in his left hand, he'd been a successful hairdresser. His career had been his passion, and the loss of his abilities grieved him. But the new house afforded them extra room, and in what was supposed to be the formal dining room, Ethan had set up his own private salon where he liked to "beautify" Sunny and Lydia. They both indulged him, even though neither of them liked being a human doll slathered with makeup and dressed in the numerous gowns he collected.

Ethan released a groan and pressed his hand to his cheek. "What's wrong?" Sunny gazed at him with concern.

"I have a toothache. It started a few days ago."

"Why didn't you tell me? Lydia or I could've already taken you to the dentist."

Ethan simply shrugged and began putting away the groceries. "It'll be fine. I'll just rinse with some saltwater."

"You've established yourself with a doctor, it's time to do the same with a dentist. I'm going to make an appointment with one Monday, and you're gonna go. You shouldn't have waited until the weekend to tell me this."

"You're my niece, not my mother."

"There's a dental office less than a mile from here. We live in a really pretty area, you should see more of it," Sunny pressed gently.

Sunny certainly understood Ethan's anxiety about getting back into a car, but the experience once she did get him to ride was just as stressful for everyone else as it was for him. On the move from Arkansas, he demanded to be sedated for the trip and rode on the backseat beneath a blanket surrounded by pillows. To her dismay, he still screamed whenever she hit a bump in the road.

"I don't want to have this discussion again, it'll make me cry," Ethan whined with dramatic flair. "I've had a bad morning. First, I stubbed my toe when I got up, and Tobi made a bed out of one of my favorite wigs. You know the one thing that will make me happy."

"Son of a bitch!"

"Oh, take it like a woman, you big titty baby."

Sunny put her hand to her burning lip. "I didn't have a mustache."

"Yes, you did." Ethan held up the wax for her to see. Sunny squinted at what looked like four blond hairs. "Now lie back, I need to do your brows."

"You know what, let's just shave them off. I'll draw them back on when I want 'em."

Ethan patted her on the shoulder. "Take comfort in the fact that they will one day fall off. When you go through menopause, your brows start coming out on your chin. Your skin will start to look like a burlap sack, but you have me to make you appear young and supple."

Sunny got up and stared at her reflection in the mirror wondering if anyone back home would even recognize her. She had been fair-haired like Lydia as a child, but as she aged, the darker it grew. At forty-one, she was growing more sensitive about the subtle lines beginning to appear around her eyes and mouth. She felt nondescript as she studied her face. "There's nothing remarkable about me."

"Bullshit. You've got the face of a model." Ethan moved behind Sunny. "I love the way your lips curve when you smile and your high cheekbones. You have the facial structure of an angel."

"My lips are too thin," Sunny said with a frown.

"Why are you so down on yourself all of the sudden?"

"Because there are mirrors everywhere in here, and the lighting shows all my flaws. I just feel old and dowdy."

"Makeover," Ethan whispered.

"What would you do?"

Ethan pushed Sunny into a chair and started yanking wigs off a row of foam heads. First, he held a fiery red one against her face. "No." Next, he put a dark brown one on her. He stood back and stared hard for a moment. "You kind of look like that country singer Shania Twain. She's very pretty."

Sunny stood and gazed at her reflection. "I don't see it, and the darker hair makes me look older."

Ethan pulled the wig off and replaced it with a dark blond one. "Oh, I'm feeling that. I have a hair color that's almost an exact match."

Sunny gazed at it for a moment. "I like it. Can you take some of my length off? I'd like it to rest just below my shoulders."

"With Lydia's help, I sure can. Then I want to tackle those brows."

Sunny nodded. "Sure, I love the sensation of having hair ripped out of my face by the roots."

Ethan grinned. "If you're really enjoying it, we can do your legs and armpits. You'll have to manage the bikini area yourself."

"Did you fail to note my sarcasm?"

"Are we doing the horror movie thing tonight?" Lydia asked as she walked into the salon.

"Yes," Ethan replied excitedly. "I ordered three new movies, and they came in yesterday. Haunted houses, haunted people, and ghostly wanderings. You don't have plans, do you?"

Lydia toyed with a bevy of nail polishes Ethan had on a tray. "I was going ballroom dancing, then to a wine tasting, but I suppose I could be persuaded to hang around here since it's movie night."

"Excellent. I need your help. I'm about to cut and color your mother's hair, and I need an extra hand."

"Dude, you need to do something about yours. You're starting to look like a lion."

Ethan released a squeal that made Sunny and Lydia jump. "Makeovers for everybody!"

Lydia stared at Sunny as the second of their movies ended later that night. "Oh, my God, we do look alike. If you would've cut your hair really short and made it messy, we'd be twins."

Sunny grabbed the popcorn bowl away from her. "You say that like it's a bad thing."

"I just never noticed it before."

Ethan was lying on the other couch and sat up. "What do I look like?"

"An old baby."

"He does not," Sunny said with a laugh.

"I'm just kidding, don't pout." Lydia winked at him. "You're a sexy beast."

Sunny admired her handiwork. She'd cut the sides short and left some length on the top. Lydia gelled it afterward, pushing the curls to the middle and the front upward. "Maybe I should quit my job and become a stylist, we could all work together."

"My salon days are over," Ethan said sadly as he lay back down.

"You can still tease and set, you used to do that for Mrs. Yoder," Sunny said, hoping to encourage him.

"She was ninety and blind as a bat. She didn't care what it looked like."

"I thought she looked a lot better when she left than she did before you got a hold of her. You cut my hair, and I love it. People at school tell me it's cool all the time." Lydia patted the couch between her and Sunny. "Come over here."

"No, y'all are just gonna pet and fawn over me to make me feel better about myself."

"Dude, I just want the caramel popcorn, I'm tired of walking over there for a handful. I heard about this next movie, it's really scary. You know you're gonna end up over here in a few minutes anyway." Lydia grinned when Ethan got up, put the movie disk in the player, and snuggled between them.

"Fine, I'll be your big protector." Ethan took a close look at Sunny's hair. "You were pretty before, but you are stunning now. I am still a master."

"Yes, you are," Sunny agreed with a smile.

"Okay, if everybody is finished being all mushy and lovey, I'm going to hit the play button," Lydia said.

"Roll it, I am ready to face the ghosts and ghouls. I am master of beauty, all things foodie. I am queen of all things mean. I am—" Ethan shrieked when a garish face appeared on the screen.

Sunny awoke when something shook her bed. In the dim light, she could see Tobi curled up in a ball sleeping nearby, but something beyond the cat caught her attention. Her sleep-addled brain tried to make sense of the dark shape that slowly moved alongside her bed. After spending the evening watching spooky things go bump in the night, her brain screamed that she was seeing something otherworldly. She sat up; shock and terror robbed her of the ability to scream. Instead when she opened her mouth, only a squeak came out.

"Mom?"

"Oh, my God! What are you doing?" Sunny bellowed at the top of her lungs.

A loud high-pitched scream came from Ethan's bedroom, and something thudded. Light came on in the hall and flooded Sunny's bedroom. Ethan stood in the doorway wielding a lamp, shade and all. "What is it? Where is it? Call 911," he screeched.

Lydia was so traumatized she could barely speak. "I...bad dream...was gonna get in bed with Mom...Tobi's in the way. I'm sorry! Okay? I'm sorry!"

Sunny inhaled sharply with a hand on her chest. "No, I'm sorry. I didn't know it was you."

"Oh, dear God, that scared the crap out of me." Ethan sagged against the doorway and hugged the lamp. "I would've shit myself if I had not done that colon cleanse earlier."

Sunny grabbed Tobi and moved her to the other side of the bed and turned down the covers. "Climb in, baby." Lydia crawled in, and Ethan followed right behind her. Sunny glared at him. "Really?"

"I have the creeps, too," he retorted.

"You left the lights on."

"Screw it, we'll all sleep better being able to see what's going to eat us. That lamp was my nightlight, and I think I broke it."

"If we're asleep, we won't see what's going to get us anyway," Sunny said as she got up. "I am so glad that I no longer sleep naked, and oh, my God, I am so relieved you don't, either." She pointed at Ethan, who had the blankets up to his chin. She switched off the lights and climbed back into bed. "At least Tobi was brave enough to sleep on her own, she left."

"No, she didn't, she just crawled between me and Uncle Ethan."

"I thought you forgot to shave your legs," Ethan quipped. "Hey, baby fur ball. You'll protect Daddy from the bad ol' demons, won't you?"

"Ethan, is that cat on my sheets?"

"Oh, don't act like you're not gonna wash them tomorrow anyway."

"Mom, do you see my point about how creepy it is to know y'all stare at me in my sleep now?"

There was a moment of silence, then Sunny said, "Yeah, but we're still gonna do it."

Lydia squirmed. "Dude, this is like a king-sized bed, you don't have to be so close."

"Then let me and Tobi be in the middle. I don't like the edge, something could reach from under and get me."

Sunny threw an arm over her eyes and listened to the pair bicker.

"You're my uncle, my protector, you can't be a poon, grow a pair."

"Well, where are your balls, butch?"

"I'm a baby dyke."

Ethan huffed. "I'd be more comfortable sleeping near the edge if at least the closet light was on."

"I have no problem with that," Sunny said as she rolled over. "You can sleep with your closet light on all night."

"After the scare you two gave me, I can't sleep alone. I doubt I'll sleep at all...for weeks even."

"Good, go make some more caramel popcorn. That stuff was off the hook." A moment or two passed by, and Ethan didn't say anything. "Are you thinking about it?" Lydia asked. The response was a soft snore. Lydia rolled on her side.

"Thanks for the knee in the butt, sweetie," Sunny mumbled against her pillow.

"At least you don't have Tobi making biscuits on your back. She needs to have her claws cut."

"That's probably Ethan."

Chapter 3

Ethan spent Sunday on the sofa with a compress on his cheek whining about his toothache. Sunny took off Monday and called the dentist's office the minute it opened. After she explained that Ethan had spent the day before in pain, the receptionist agreed to fit them in as soon as possible. Sunny knew that Ethan was genuinely miserable because he didn't fuss about going, nor did he resort to any of his dramatic antics on the five-minute ride.

"They need a new decorator," Ethan whispered as they sat in the waiting room. "I hate cream-colored paint, it looks like white stained by nicotine. Plastic plants, how gauche." He snatched at a leaf and squealed. "It's real! Hide the evidence of my vandalism."

Sunny took the leaf with a sigh and tossed it into a trash can. "I'm going to tell the dentist you accosted her plant. She's probably not going to give you any Novocain now."

"A woman? Oh, I feel so much better, they tend to be gentle. Although you blow a hole in that theory. I remember how roughly you handled me when I cut my hand with a kitchen knife."

"You were running in circles screaming hysterically and bleeding all over the place. I had to tackle you to put pressure on it."

A young woman walked into the waiting area wearing dark blue scrubs and called Ethan's name.

"That's me," Ethan said as he got up and waved. He took two steps before he realized that Sunny wasn't behind him. He turned and glared at her.

"Seriously?" she asked. "Lydia even thinks she's too old for me to accompany her."

Ethan stamped his foot. "Come!"

"You are such a pansy," she whispered as she followed.

"I'm Courtney, one of Dr. Savino's assistants," the woman said as she led Ethan and Sunny into a room. Sunny sat out of the way while Ethan climbed into the dentist's chair. "Tell me what's going on, Mr. Chase."

"I've been having a toothache for about a week now, but this weekend, the pain became unbearable. I can hardly brush on the left side of my mouth, and my gums are swollen."

"Have you been able to identify which tooth it is that hurts, or does the pain radiate?" Courtney asked as she reclined the chair.

"I don't know which one it is. My jaw just burns and aches on the bottom left side."

Courtney pulled on a pair of gloves and picked up a mouth mirror. "Let me have a look." Her brow rose, then furrowed as she made an inspection. Ethan nearly came out of the chair when she stuck her finger in and poked around. "I'm gonna have Dr. Savino come have a look. She'll be here in just a minute."

"Did you see the look on her face? There's something terrible in my mouth," Ethan said worriedly.

Sunny nodded. "Yeah, your tongue, and it's always loaded with bullshit."

"Is this your idea of being supportive?"

"You were distracted there for a moment, so I'm gonna go with yes," Sunny said smugly.

"Hello, I'm Dr. Savino," a woman wearing a pair of orange cat ears said cheerily as she walked into the room.

Ethan gazed up at her with a frown. "Halloween is still weeks out, you're way ahead of the game."

Noel smiled at him. "I specialize in pediatric dentistry, but I assure you that I'm qualified to take care of adults, as well."

"She's got both of your personalities covered. Can I pick a dentist or what?"

Ethan continued to frown. "That's my niece who has decided to become a comedian in my time of dire suffering."

"Sunny Chase," she said as she stood and extended her hand.

"A pleasure to meet you." Noel took Sunny's hand. "I'm so glad you came in today."

"I hate to point out that the patient is in the chair," Ethan said grumpily.

Noel turned and smiled at him. "Now that the introductions are done, you have my full attention. I'm just going to wash up while we discuss what's going on with you." She stepped over to the sink and began to soap her hands liberally. "Do you remember biting down on something that hurt, or did the pain come on gradually?"

"I just woke up one morning with my jaw on fire."

"Let me have a look," Noel said as she pulled on a pair of gloves and picked up a mirror.

Ethan shrank back. "Aren't you going to take those ears off?"

"The headband is keeping my hair out of my face. Does the tickle monster need to come out to get you to open up?" Ethan's mouth popped open like a trap door. Noel gently maneuvered her mirror around and nodded. "I see what you're talking about, Courtney, good catch."

"Is it cancer?" Ethan asked as soon as the instrument cleared his lips.

Noel shook her head. "There's something protruding out of your gum, and the tissue around it is swollen. I suspect that's what's causing the issue here. Have you eaten anything like nuts, popcorn, or maybe fish with bones in it lately?"

"We had popcorn Saturday, but it hurt before then," Ethan said.

"But we did have fish a week and a half ago," Sunny added. "You broiled the bass that Roger sent home with me."

"I can see just the tip of it poking out. I'd like to see if I can give it a tug, but you're obviously having a lot of pain with it,"

Noel explained. "Since the tissue around it is inflamed, I'm not sure it will deaden enough, so I'm going to suggest laughing gas. Have you ever had nitrous oxide before?"

"Oh, yes, anytime I've had dental work done. I'm ready for the pig nose, Doctor. My favorite flavor is cherry."

Noel nodded at Courtney. "Go ahead and set it up." Then she turned her attention to Sunny. "How did y'all hear about us?"

"We don't live far from here, I pass your office every day," Sunny said and noticed again the lingering look that Noel gave her.

"We must be practically neighbors then because my house is about six blocks from here." Noel switched on the gas once Ethan's mask was in place. "Just take a couple of deep breaths and relax, Mr. Chase."

Sunny's lesbian radar went off the minute Noel walked into the room. She was feminine at first glance, but the way she moved whispered butch. Her chestnut brown hair was short in back, but the top and sides held back by the cat ears appeared longer. Her heavily lidded green eyes gave her a sexy, sultry look until she smiled and the dimples popped out. Sunny hated to see Noel's face covered by the mask she slipped over her nose and mouth. Her lips were full and looked incredibly kissable.

"Oh, kitty kitty," Ethan softly cooed. "You look like Tobi, except her ears are gray. She has a pink and black nose. Your muzzle is blue, but you have the same big green eyes."

"That's his cat," Sunny explained.

"She's a...sport cat," Ethan continued, "because she's...sporty. She doesn't like Sunny because Sunny wants to put her in the washing machine."

"That was a joke," Sunny clarified when Noel and Courtney turned to her. "He thinks her saliva has bleach in...never mind."

Ethan continued to ramble. "She's been bitchy lately because she hasn't had sex in like forever."

"He's still talking about the cat," Sunny added quickly.

Noel motioned for something from Courtney. "Mr. Chase, I'm going to—"

"I took off her mustache."

Sunny cleared her throat. "Tobi has a...too much facial fur."

"You're a lesbian, aren't you?" Ethan squinted up at Noel. "You have very nice brows, kitty kitty."

"Thank you. Now I'm going to put a block between your teeth that will keep your mouth open while I work."

"Will that shut him up?" Sunny asked.

Ethan reached for Noel. "I won't bite. You have really big hands, but that's a good thing for a lesbian to have, right?"

Courtney whirled around to hide her laughter. Sunny sank deeper into her chair and whispered, "Oh, my dear God."

Noel fought to retain her composure. "Thank you," she said with a laugh.

"You're really hung if you know what I mean."

Noel's eyes teared as she fought to keep from cackling. "Courtney, you wanna help me out with the bite block...Courtney?"

Noel's assistant was doubled over.

"Where is it? I'll shove it in his trap," Sunny said as she stood. "I'm so sorry."

"It's okay," Noel said as Courtney inserted the block. "I needed that laugh."

Sunny's face felt like it was on fire while she watched Noel work. "I'd like to blame his behavior on the gas, but he isn't a whole lot different when he's completely lucid."

Noel chuckled while focused on her task. "You should meet my mother. If you ever watched *The Golden Girls*, then you'll understand what I mean when I say my mom is Sophia Petrillo on steroids. This little rascal is really stuck in here." Noel lowered the head of the chair farther to give her a better angle. All the while Ethan was attempting to talk. "I'll have it out in just a minute."

Sunny stood again and tried to see what was going on in Ethan's mouth. "Take your time, I'm enjoying the serenity. Is there any way I can get one of those blocks and some of that gas to take home?"

Noel glanced at her. "If that were possible, my parents' house would be a lot more pleasant. My dad would throw a parade in my honor." She sighed when Ethan groaned. "I'm sorry for taking so long, Mr. Chase. It's wedged beneath a tooth, but it's just about to—ah." Noel held up her forceps to reveal a quarter-inch sliver of bone. "I'm gonna give you some fresh air now, and your head will begin to clear."

"So the offending object was a fishbone, and his teeth are fine?" Sunny asked.

Noel removed her mask. "I took a cursory look around in there, and his teeth appear to be okay, but X-rays tell the real story. I'm going to send some rinse home with you that'll help his gums heal quickly. If he'd like a thorough checkup after he feels better, I'd be more than happy to see y'all again."

As soon as Courtney removed the block, Ethan started to yammer. "Your hands are huge. Sunny, ask her out right now."

"Please put the bite block back in," Sunny said as she put a hand over her face.

"I was trying to help," Ethan snapped, then whimpered as he pressed his hand to his cheek. "From cloud nine, I could clearly see that she was flirting with you."

Sunny slammed her car door. "I don't need your help in that department."

"Oh," Ethan said with derisive laugh, "yes, you do. Your nether regions are probably boarded up like an abandoned mine. Dr. Kitty would be the perfect miner, she's even got a special light."

"I wish I was more like you. You used to pick up a man with a snap of your fingers when you wanted to. I just get tongue tied when the chance to make a move is presented." Sunny turned the engine in her Jeep. "You, of course, stomped right in the middle of any chance I had back there."

"No, you did that when you took off running."

"I know you," Harper said as she walked up to Lydia on the school courtyard at lunch. "I'm outta projects, I hope you don't get in trouble again."

"Me too." Lydia jerked a thumb at the boy standing next to her. "This is Brenden."

"She knows, we've gone to school together since junior high. Hey, Harper," Brenden said with a smile. "How's Corey?"

"Still mean and stuck-up. I can't believe you dated her."

Brenden shrugged. "She's hot. I miss your grandma's cannolis, though."

"Dude, don't talk about her grandma like that," Lydia said with a laugh that ended suddenly when Brenden didn't catch the joke.

Harper chuckled more at the blank expression on Brenden's face than Lydia's quip.

"Hey, we're going to the Snack Shop after school, you wanna come?" Lydia asked Harper. "I'll buy you a hot dog or nachos for being so nice to me the other night after I got paint on your sweatshirt."

"I don't have a car. I ride back and forth to school with my cousins."

"You can ride with me. I'll take you home after. Where do you live?"

"On Capital Heights."

Lydia wrinkled her nose. "I don't know why I asked because I have no idea where everything is. I'm still learning my way around Baton Rouge."

"It's in the Garden District about two miles from where you live," Brenden said.

"Well, cool." Lydia smiled at Harper. "You want a ride?"

"Okay," Harper said with a nod. "Where do you want me to meet you?"

"I'm parked near the back doors of the gym," Lydia said as the bell rang.

"I'll see you then. Bye."

Lydia watched Harper run off until Brenden nudged her. "You know she's straight, right?" he said as he and Lydia went the opposite direction.

"Yeah, I figured."

"I mean, there's rumors because she's not real girly and she's tight with her aunt who's gay, but they aren't true, according to Corey. She's cool, though. Sometimes we'd hang out when Corey was being a bitch."

"You like her?"

Brenden shrugged. "She's nerdy, but she's kinda cute. Not my type, though, and I've got a girlfriend. I'm just dropping the info in case you've got a thing for her."

"I don't," Lydia lied.

"That's good because she's a Savino, even though her last name is Guidry. The Savinos have a rep for taking care of each other. Mason nearly beat my ass when me and Corey broke up, and I was the one that got dumped."

"You look like shit."

"Thanks, Mom," Noel said with a frown as she sank down at Inez's kitchen table. "I've come to beg for food, I'm too tired to cook."

"You don't cook. You pour cereal into a bowl."

"Well, I'm outta milk, and I was too beat to stop at the store. What's in the pot?"

"I made stew because I have no idea when your father will be home. He and Jeff went fishing again. That's all he does since he retired. Does he fix the broken spindle on the porch? No, he rides around in a boat all day drinking beer."

"Tell Matt to fix the porch."

"No, it's Joe's job. I'm gonna tell him that when he gets home." Inez ladled the stew into two bowls and set them on the table. Then she grabbed a bottle of wine, a couple of glasses, and some of the bread that she'd already sliced from a French loaf. "This is nice, just us girls."

"How was your day?"

Inez sighed as she sat down. "Interesting. Greg came home, and he has what can loosely be described as a woman with him. They came over earlier today, and he brought me a bunch of that homemade jam I like from that market in the country he goes to. He said he got a flat tire on the road, and that woman...her name is Rhonda or Rhoda or something like that. Anyway, Greg said he couldn't figure out how to get the spare from under his new truck. Rhonda stopped, got the tire out, and changed it. You should see the man, he's looking at that woman all starry-eyed, and she's as ugly as belching in church."

"Mom," Noel said, glancing at the screen door behind them. "The door is open, and your voice carries, he might hear you."

Inez waved her off. "I don't think we're gonna see Greg for a while the way those two were carrying on. Noel, she looks like Danny DeVito, I swear. The only thing missing is the receding hairline and the cigar. When you get home, I want you to get on your computer and see if DeVito has a twin sister because if he does, Greg is dating her."

Noel laughed as she tried to blow on a spoonful of soup. "You're so mean."

"Wait till you see her, you'll see I'm telling you the truth. If that woman can get a man, then Mary can, too." Inez poked Noel in the arm. "And you can get a good woman."

"I met a cute one today, but she was the niece of a patient, so I couldn't unleash my powers of persuasion on her."

Inez sucked her teeth. "Try using your powers for good for a change. I think you've proven to yourself that you can catch them like flypaper. Don't let what happened with Brenna make you feel like you don't have a lot to offer the right one."

"The breakup didn't damage me, Momma." Noel licked her lips as she stared at her dinner. "I'm tired of always picking the wrong one. My hormones ruled me with Julianna and…Amber," she admitted with a sigh. "With Brenna, I used my head, and things still turned out bad. Now here I am at thirty-five with three failed relationships behind me. Technically, I wasn't married to any of them, but I still feel divorced. You and Dad are still together, Matt and Lauren are still going strong, Mary would still be with Dave had he not embezzled a shitload of money and gone to prison, then there's me on the third strike."

"Eat, I'll do the talking." Inez sat back with a piece of bread and a philosophical look on her face. Now that you kids are grown, I find myself with a lot of time on my hands, so I spend some of it on the porch. Lately, I've been watching Jolene's mutt and the Sutters' cat."

"You need a hobby."

"I told you to eat." Inez cleared her throat. "Listen to what I have to say because it's brilliant, and one day, I'm gonna write a book. Dr. Phil's gonna wanna interview me, although I'd prefer

Dr. Oz, then I see that Oz taking me to dinner and we...anyway. So I watch the dog. Jolene puts him out, and he takes a crap on Greg's lawn, then he goes back to Jolene's and begs to get in. When Jolene is in her yard, the dog is always by her side, and he's thrilled with any affection she decides to show him. Now the Sutters' cat goes outside and does its thing, he doesn't really care if he gets back into the house or not. When Donna has her coffee in the afternoons on the porch, the cat will come by and allow her to pat him on the head exactly three times, he buffs her leg, climbs up on the railing, and takes a nap. People behave like dogs and cats in relationships, that's the cat/dog dynamic, you follow me so far?"

Noel nodded slowly. "You wanna get nasty with Dr. Oz, and you need a hobby."

"Okay, for your sake, I'm going to pretend that you're not a smartass like your father. He's a dog. He likes to be close all the time. The other day, he wanted me to sit in the garage and watch him change the oil on the lawnmower. He wants constant affection, and I'm not talking sex. He wants to hear me say I love him a dozen times a day, and he wants to be needed, even though he never does what I ask him to. Now Matt's wife, Lauren, is a cat. She needs her space, and when Matt invades it, he gets the claw. She welcomes affection when she wants it, and she'll give it when she's in the mood. But Lauren doesn't need or want Matt around all the time, she's independent."

Noel bit the inside of her cheek to keep from laughing. "So...are you saying that cats need to be with cats and dogs need to be with dogs?"

Inez nodded.

"So what are you?"

"I'm a cat," Inez said as though the answer should've been obvious.

"But you just said Dad's a dog, and according to your dynamic, dogs and cats shouldn't be together."

Inez threw up her hands. "Exactly, and that is why I want to scratch your father to pieces all the time. That's why Matt and Lauren fight so much 'cause Matt's a dog like his father."

Noel chuckled as she pinched the skin of her forehead. "But y'all are still together."

"That don't mean we're happy," Inez said while wagging her finger. "It took me years to train your father, and I'm still working with that bad dog. If I would've picked a cat, I wouldn't have had to go to that trouble. You're a cat, Noel, you need a cat. Brenna and the rest of them were all dogs. Get yourself a cat, preferably an Italian one that can cook."

Noel held up both hands. "Are these big?"

"What're you asking me?"

"Are my hands too big? Are they outta proportion with the rest of me?"

Inez shook her head and rolled her eyes. "You're a cat with the attention span of a terrier."

Chapter 4

Noel pulled up to the curb where Harper was standing Friday morning and rolled down her window. "Hey, are Mason and Corey running late?"

"I don't ride with them anymore, so I don't have to leave as early. It sucked getting up before dawn just so Mason could get his protein smoothie."

Noel made a face. "It also sucks not having your own car. I bet that graduation present can't come soon enough."

"So true." Harper spotted Lydia's white truck coming up the street. "Hey, stick around and meet my new friend, she's family."

Noel pulled her car into the driveway and got out just as Harper climbed into the passenger's seat of the truck. "Hey, I'm Noel, Harper's aunt," she said as she walked over to them.

"Nice to meet you, I'm Lydia, Harper's chauffeur."

Noel cocked her head as she gazed at the young girl. "Have we met?"

"I don't think so," Lydia said.

"You must remind me of someone." Noel pulled her wallet out of her pocket and slipped Harper a twenty. "Give that to Lydia for gas."

Harper handed it back. "We have a deal. I buy snacks after school, and she drives. I still have money from my summer job, and Lydia eats like a bird."

Noel crumpled the bill up and tossed it at Lydia. "Oh, look what you found. Stick it in your gas tank, and drive very carefully with my baby. It was nice to meet you."

"You too," Lydia said.

"Love you," Harper called after Noel as she walked back to her car.

"Your aunt's pretty cool, and she's hot. If she had longer hair, she'd have that whole Lara Croft thing going on—not like Angelina Jolie, but more like the character in the game."

"And she's eighteen years older than you, technically old enough to be your mother," Harper said with a laugh. "You're outta luck there."

"Dude, I was thinking more about my mom, she's single."

"I love my aunt, but she's not girlfriend material. She's a player. My nana calls Noel coochie catcher behind her back because she catches them and turns them loose."

"Ah," Lydia said with disappointment. "I want my mom to be with someone that will treasure her."

Harper smiled at her. "I think it's sweet that you wanna hook her up."

Lydia was quiet for a moment, then said, "She should be happy. Mom really hasn't been in a relationship since like forever."

Harper's brow rose. "Is she like Noel?"

"Oh, no, she dates, but nothing ever seems to work out. She says it's because we moved so much."

"Are you here temporarily?" Harper asked with concern.

"No, this is supposed to be our last stop. Mom wants to settle here, and she wants me to go to LSU."

Harper was just getting to know Lydia, but she'd already ranked her as a good friend, and the prospect of her moving away was already unsettling. "Where's Brenden?"

"He finally got his car running, so it's just us from now on."

"I like him, but I'm kinda glad. We never really got a chance to talk because he couldn't be quiet."

"You don't know how many times I just wanted to punch him in the forehead. We, like, never got a word in edgewise.

We've been riding together for a week, and this is the most we've talked. Do you have plans for tonight?"

"We're going to watch Mason play football, but I'd much rather spend time with you."

"We can hang out at my place, but I need to warn you that my uncle loves to dress up like old movie stars. He might be in drag when we get there."

"I can't wait to see that," Harper said with a laugh. "I've tried to talk Noel into taking me to drag shows, but they're all in bars, so I'm outta luck."

Lydia breathed a sigh. "I'm so glad you're cool with it. I haven't had friends over since we moved here. He's totally dramatic. Last week when we had that thunderstorm, he and his cat camped out under a mattress in the hallway. He bitched for a solid hour about how crazy we were for not getting under it with him. Mom had to threaten to throw out his nail polish to get him to shut up."

"You lied! Donovan next door said there was indeed fennel at the grocery store. He saw it today when he went shopping."

Sunny had barely made it in the door that evening when Ethan began his assault. "Donovan is half-blind, he thought Tobi was a Chihuahua. Just because they had it today doesn't mean they had it when I went. If you're about to tell me that's what's for dinner, I'm going to McDonald's."

Ethan stood up straight. "That last statement erased all the shame I felt for stealing your capri pants." He stepped out from behind the kitchen island to show that he'd stuffed his ass in her favorite pair with the cargo pockets.

Sunny covered her eyes. "Your bulge is showing!"

"Your breasts bulge under your shirt!"

"My shirt! *My* shirt! I don't wear your shirts, and I don't want to see your business in my pants. I thought we agreed that you would stay out of my closet."

"I was putting away your laundry and saw these. I just couldn't resist." Ethan turned his back to Sunny. "I don't have any panty lines. Is my ass cute or what?"

Sunny clenched her fists. "Keep the pants. Where is Lydia?"

"She called to check in after school and said she and a friend were going to some Halloween store. The friend is staying for dinner, so they'll be here then."

Sunny tossed her work bag into the foyer, then returned to the kitchen where she watched Ethan season a large bowl of hamburger. "Is this a new friend?"

"I think so. Her name is Harper, and I haven't heard Lydia mention her before."

"I haven't, either," Sunny said with a smile. "Good, I'm glad she's socializing. Will you be wearing those pants for dinner?"

Ethan jutted his chin. "Don't be jealous that I'm rocking them."

"Honey, you should've looked at more than your ass in the mirror. You have a camel toe."

"This house blocks out the sun," Harper said as she hopped out of Lydia's truck.

"Mom and Ethan wanted a big one. Mom wanted enough space for Ethan to set up his salon, even though he no longer does that kind of work. He says he wanted extra room in case Mom falls in love, so she and her girlfriend can have their privacy. But I think he's just really kinda scared that if Mom met someone she wanted to live with, the new girlfriend would want him out."

"Would your mom ever ask him to leave?"

"Never, we're the only family she's got. She and Ethan argue like an old married couple, but they love each other to pieces."

After what Lydia had told her, Harper was looking forward to seeing Liz Taylor or Audrey Hepburn. But when they stepped inside, she was greeted by a small man wearing an oversized gray sweatshirt that looked like a dress and a pair of black leggings. His feet were bare, and his toenails were painted dark red.

"Uncle Ethan, this is Harper Guidry."

"How lovely to meet you," he said as he rushed over, took Harper's hand, and kissed it.

"It's a pleasure to meet you too, Mr. Ethan."

"Oh, no, you call me just plain ol' Ethan. We're having burgers tonight, but if you're a vegetarian, I'll whip up something else."

"No, a burger sounds great to me. Can I help with anything?" Harper asked.

Ethan's eyes grew huge as he slapped his hand against his cheek. "You're so well mannered."

Lydia rolled her eyes when Harper grinned at her. "Oh, and that's Tobi, our cat, over there on the hearth."

"You have a fireplace in the kitchen, how cool!" Harper exclaimed as she walked over to where it took up one corner and was flanked by French doors. "This house is beautiful."

"Thank you."

Harper turned toward the new voice as Sunny walked into the room with a smile and extended her hand. "I'm Sunny Chase, it's nice to meet you."

"You too." Harper looked back and forth between Lydia and Sunny. "Except for the hair, y'all look like twin sisters, not mother and daughter."

Sunny laughed. "Oh, I like you."

Lydia grabbed Harper by the arm. "Come on, let me show you around."

Compared to the garage apartment she shared with her mother behind her grandparents' house, Harper felt like she was in the Taj Mahal. Their footsteps echoed on the tile floor as they walked through the living room past a seating area that contained two tan L-shaped sofas and a big-screen TV.

"There's two rooms upstairs and a sitting area, but they're unfinished, so we use them for storage. The people that had it before were renovating it and ended up going bankrupt, I think. Mom's and Ethan's rooms are at the end of the hall, and they both have private bathrooms. I'm stuck with the guest bath. But that's okay because check out my room."

Harper's brow shot into her hairline. The room was split-level. Lydia's bed and dresser were on the elevated part. She had a desk and her own private door that opened onto the patio. "Is your mom or Ethan looking to adopt another kid?" Harper said as she twirled around and walked over to a framed poster on the wall. "*Wicked*! Have you seen it?"

Lydia nodded. "We saw it off Broadway, but it's my dream to go to New York and see it there."

"Mine too," Harper said with a sigh, "but I'd settle for off Broadway. *The Addams Family Musical* is coming here in November, Noel said she'd take me. We should all go."

"That'd be cool." Inside, Lydia was dancing over the fact that they had yet another thing in common. They had so little time alone to really talk. The ride to school was short, and Brenden was with them almost all the time talking his head off. But Lydia was able to find out that she and Harper listened to the same type of music and that she loved Halloween.

"Eighties movies," Harper exclaimed as she looked at Lydia's collection. "And you've got all the *Shreks*." She pulled a case from the shelf and held it up. "*The Breakfast Club*, a total classic. This is one of my all-time favorite flicks."

"Everything on that shelf is my favorite. I love horror movies, too. We have a cabinet full of them in the living room."

"I watch those with Noel sometimes. My mother hates them," Harper said as she replaced the movie case.

"Lydia, I need your assistance in the kitchen, please," Ethan called out.

"Be right there," Lydia yelled. "His left hand is kinda messed up, so I'm his southpaw."

Harper followed Lydia into the kitchen and watched as Lydia took over slicing an onion. "What can I do?"

"May I put you in charge of the tomato?"

"Absolutely." She accepted a cutting board and a knife from Ethan and got to work.

"Harper says *The Addams Family Musical* is coming here in November," Lydia said as her eyes began to tear.

Harper smiled. "My aunt and I are planning to go. I think we all should."

"I'm a homebody, but Sunny would love that." Ethan set the hamburger buns in the oven to toast. "She needs to get out more and meet people."

"Harper's aunt is gay," Lydia added. "She and Mom would probably make good friends."

Ethan swooped over to Harper. "Is she single?"

"She's all about the booty. Noel doesn't do relationships."

"Who doesn't?" Sunny asked as she walked in with a tray of grilled patties.

"We were just talking about Harper's single, gay aunt," Ethan replied with a big grin. "I think I'd like to meet her. How old is she?"

"Thirty-five. She's a dentist," Harper said.

Ethan and Sunny exchanged glances. "Does she wear cat ears and have big green eyes like you do?" Ethan asked.

Harper nodded. "When she has young patients. Have you met her already?"

"Oh, I think we have," Sunny said as her face colored. "Ethan called her names and said things about her hands."

"Dude, why?" Lydia demanded.

Ethan shrugged. "I had gas."

Chapter 5

Mary walked onto the porch where Noel and Inez sat together on the swing. "How do I look?" She struck a pose in a sleek black cocktail dress.

"Like a hooker."

"Momma!" Noel said and burst out laughing. She waved at Mary, who was snarling. "You look fantastic."

"You do," Inez agreed with a chuckle. "I'm just playing with you, baby. That dress really shows off your beautiful figure."

"I've eaten nothing but celery for lunch this whole week so I could fit in this thing." Mary ran a hand over her hip. "I can't remember the last time I really dressed up."

"Where is this dinner party you're attending?" Noel asked.

"At Vincent's new house. I'm sure he invited me because I spent more time with his wife, Grace, planning this event than I did actually working. So I'm going to hobnob with my boss's wealthy friends and maybe I'll meet a single millionaire looking for a wife to lavish his riches on."

"Work it, sis. You going stag?"

Mary nodded as she dropped her phone into her purse. "Grace's sister is gonna pick me up. She doesn't live far from here, and she doesn't drink, so I'll have a designated driver. Momma, I told Harper to be home no later than ten since I'm going to be out tonight."

"I'll make sure she's in the nest. If not, Noel will hunt her down."

The three of them watched a silver Mercedes pull into the driveway. "That's my ride," Mary said as she kissed her mother on the cheek. "Wish me luck."

"She doesn't need any luck in that dress," Noel said with a smile.

They waved as the car drove away, and a loud cackle of laughter rang out. Inez jerked a thumb at Greg's house. "That's her, the DeVito woman. Go hide in the bushes and look at her."

"I am not."

Inez gave Noel a nudge. "I'll go with you. The gardenia is big enough to hide both of us. I know because when I need to get away from your father, that's where I go." She grabbed Noel's hand and stood. "Don't make me go to the bush alone."

"Momma, I'm not gonna spy on Greg from the shrubs," Noel protested but was ignored while being dragged like a rag doll to a cave-like opening between two large gardenia bushes.

"Have a seat, it's easier to look through my foliage window."

There was just enough light coming from Greg's patio for Noel to see inside the nest. Her mouth sagged open. "You have a bench in here?" she squeaked in a whisper as she snatched up a plastic bag. "And cigarettes! You said you quit."

"You wanna shut up?" Inez took a seat and patted the bench. "Sit."

Noel's foot bumped something as she sat. She scooped up a bottle of bourbon, half empty. "Oh, my God, you've built a den of iniquity in the hedge."

"Your father's a pig when it comes to booze. If I want a drink, I have to hide it." Inez snatched the bottle from Noel's hand. "You tell anybody about this, I'll cut you—from the will, I don't mean I'll shank you. Now look."

Danny DeVito in female form truly was sitting on Greg's patio while he stood at the grill. "Oh…wow," Noel whispered.

"She could be DeVito's sister, but her last name is Hudson. That don't mean anything, though. She coulda been married before."

Noel shook her head. "I can't believe you hide in this bush and spy on Greg."

"I spy on everybody. That's how I know you've been slinging that cooch all over the place."

"I have not!"

"What? You don't know how to whisper? Hush. How do you explain all the cars in your driveway? How do you keep all those women separate? Don't some of them show up unexpected?"

"I do *not* sleep with all of them. Sometimes, I may have a woman over for dinner, but that doesn't mean we have sex."

"Noel, you don't cook, you make them eat cereal?"

"I pick up food. Roman's has some pretty delicious dishes."

Inez smacked her lips. "I tried the eggplant once, but it was too salty." She lit up a cigarette and exhaled a lungful of smoke. "Find the right woman, settle down, and make your momma happy."

"It's not like I don't want to. There aren't that many stray cats out there, and the ones I do find, I don't wanna keep."

"What about that girl you brought to dinner a month or two ago?"

"She had chronic bad breath and was offended when I offered her a free cleaning and exam," Noel said with a sigh.

"What about the one you used to jog with?"

"She had big feet. They sounded like flippers smacking the pavement. I couldn't deal with that."

Inez sucked her teeth. "Greg is almost fifty, and now look what he's been forced to work with. Danny DeVito is cute in an impish sorta way, but he's hideous as a woman. You're gonna be stuck with something like that if you don't stop being so picky. You're four years from forty, it don't get no easier after that, let me tell you."

"Momma, I'm thirty-five."

"Whatever."

"Greg is fifty-five."

"Shut up."

Harper was thoroughly enjoying herself with the Chases and their crazy conversations. Ethan had started them off by bringing up a show he'd watched recently on the Bermuda Triangle, and they all discussed their own theories about the disappearance of planes and boats. Then the conversation veered into horror movies. Harper couldn't help but laugh at the absurdity of the debate over whether a zombie apocalypse could actually occur.

Ethan shook his head. "I just have to agree with Lydia, it's plausible that something could infect the brain and cause a zombie-like state."

"Yes, it's called laughing gas. Poor Dr. Savino had no idea what kind of monster she was going to make with that," Sunny said.

Lydia narrowed her eyes at Ethan. "What exactly did you say to Noel?"

"Don't you dare repeat it," Sunny said when Ethan opened his mouth. "My bad for bringing it up. Harper, tell us your zombie theories."

"I don't know of any, but I'm sure there are psychiatric diseases out there that cause some sort of zombie-like state, but causing them to eat people is way out there."

Lydia folded her arms. "What if the disease originates in a group of cannibals?"

Sunny smiled at Harper. "As you can see, we watch too many scary movies. It's kind of a tradition we do on the weekends. Zombies are what's in now, so we've been watching the movies and TV shows. What's your favorite form of mindless entertainment?"

"I like the creepy stuff, too. I watch *The Walking Dead* at my aunt's house because my mom won't watch with me, and it's really no fun watching alone. Nana—my grandma—says Noel is macabre because Halloween is her favorite holiday." Harper laughed. "We're really nerds because we love to get the ceramic haunted houses from the craft store and paint them. The village we've made is huge. Noel ran outta space on her mantel, so she bought a table that we set up. That's probably what we'll end up doing tomorrow." She glanced at her watch. "Oh, man, I told my mom I'd be home by ten."

Lydia checked the time on her phone. "That's no problem, it's only nine thirty. I can have you there in five minutes."

"I wanted to be able to clean up," Harper said as she stood and began picking up their dessert plates before Sunny stopped her.

"I've got this. If you start hanging around here, and I hope you will," Sunny said with a smile, "I might let you pick up then."

Lydia stood and pulled her keys out of her pocket with a grin. "If I'm lucky, it'll all be done by the time I get back."

"Harper, drop Lydia off at your house, and you come back here," Ethan said.

"Thank y'all for inviting me to dinner. It was great, and I enjoyed the zombie discussions." Harper hugged Ethan and Sunny.

"Next time, we'll talk more about you. I'd like to hear all about your family," Sunny said as she stood and walked the girls to the door.

"Okay, that's a scary movie in itself," Harper said with a laugh. "Good night."

When the door closed, Ethan chuckled softly. "That dentist is on your mind," he sang.

"I won't deny it." Sunny scooped up the dessert dishes and took them to the sink. "I'd actually thought about making an appointment for myself just to have an excuse to see her again. Harper may provide the opportunity, though."

"I really like that young lady. Lydia does, too, but in an entirely different way." Ethan stabbed a finger on the counter. "Mark my words right here."

"I noticed." Sunny rinsed off the dishes and stuck them into the dishwasher. "Both of them were giving each other the eye."

"Your mom and Ethan are really nice," Harper said as Lydia drove her home. "Ethan totally cracks me up."

"He was playing it cool tonight because he just met you. Once he gets comfortable, he'll be dressed in all kinds of crazy stuff. He'll sing, too, and it is *bad*. Mom runs out of the room, and I just plug my buds into my ears and blast the music."

"Hey, if we paint the Halloween houses tomorrow, you wanna come over? It's probably not your thing, but it's kinda fun, and you're good with a brush."

"Yeah," Lydia said with a shrug. "Call me."

"You'll probably end up meeting most of my family. Nana's nosy, she'll ask you a million questions, but she's sweet. Pops, that's my grandfather, will talk your ear off about sports, and if you don't like football, don't admit it. He thinks that if you fully understand the game, you'll learn to love it, so you'll get a complete lesson."

"I do hate football," Lydia whispered.

Harper gazed at her with a smile. "Me too. I won't tell if you don't."

Lydia turned into the driveway and asked, "What time do you think y'all will do the Halloween house thing?"

"It won't be early. Noel likes to sleep in on the weekends, so probably after lunch sometime."

"Good, I don't like to get out of bed until then, either."

Harper climbed out of the truck and was about to say something else when suddenly Noel stepped out of the shrubs. Harper yelped, and Lydia screamed, which in turn caused Noel to scream. "You scared the shit outta me. What's wrong with you, Harper?" Noel ran both hands through her hair.

Harper swatted at her. "You scared me. Why were you in the bushes?"

"I...uh...I thought I heard something. It sounded like one of those really annoying squawking birds, and I was going to set the shrubs on fire to run it outta there." Noel pursed her lips and nodded. "That's it." She looked into the cab of the truck. "Hey, Lydia, sorry about scaring you."

Lydia nodded. "That's...it's okay."

"I invited Lydia to paint the village houses with us tomorrow," Harper said. "You have to buy us pizza since you nearly made us shit our pants."

Noel looked confused. "Did we make plans to do that?"

Harper nodded. "Just now."

"Okay, pizza and painting tomorrow. We'll have to go get the new models first." Noel smiled as she regarded Lydia. "We can pick you up around noon."

"That's cool."

Harper dragged Noel out of the way. "Thanks for tonight, I had fun. I'm glad you're coming tomorrow."

"Me too." Lydia waved when Harper closed the door and backed out of the driveway.

Harper glared at Noel. "You made me fart in front of her! I may have really shit my pants." She turned and marched off.

"I really am sorry," Noel called after her.

The sound of snickering rose with smoke from the hedge. "I told you not to step out."

"Thanks, Mom."

Chapter 6

"I've cleaned the bathrooms and changed all the sheets. Do you have anything else you want me to do before I shower?" Lydia asked as Sunny mopped the kitchen.

"Yes, Ethan wants a box he stored upstairs, but he can't find it. Would you go up there with your excellent little peepers and see if you can find it? It's marked 'old wigs.'"

"Sure," Lydia said as she turned to go.

Sunny nudged her in the butt with the mop. "Hey, what're you in such a hurry to do today?"

"Harper and her aunt are gonna pick me up to paint the village thing." Lydia frowned and rubbed her wet shorts. "I was thinking about inviting Harper to watch a movie night, is that okay?"

"Sure," Sunny said with a smile.

"Can she spend the night if she wants?"

"I don't see why not." Sunny returned to mopping, then abruptly stopped. "Baby, is Harper—"

"She's straight and just a friend." Lydia held up both hands. "If she stays, we're gonna sleep on the couches in the living room."

Sunny nodded with a smile. "Good, you can scare her in the middle of the night instead of me."

"Or we all may end up in your bed again." Lydia dodged the mop with a laugh. "You gotta be faster to catch the baby dyke twice in one day." She bolted when Sunny took off after her.

"That's right, get your baby butt up those stairs," Sunny called after her with a laugh. "If the floor wouldn't have been wet, I would've had you."

"In your dreams, old lady."

"It's on," Sunny said and dropped the mop before she tore up the stairs.

Ethan in his salon looked up at the ceiling when he heard what sounded like a herd of buffalo stampeding above. Doors slammed, and there was more stomping and banging. He smiled when he heard muffled laughing and screaming.

"Nice house," Noel said as she pulled into the Chases' driveway.

"Yeah, it's really cool on the inside. You should come in and meet Lydia's mom. Actually, I think you already have. She came to your office," Harper said as she got of Noel's car.

Noel climbed out, only paying half attention. "What's her dad do?"

"Lydia lives with her mom and uncle, there's no dad," Harper said as she walked toward the front door. "Her mom's gay, too, and—"

The door flew open, and a very short version of Cher stood smiling at them, and he pointed at Noel. "I know you."

"I know you, too, and let me just say that you were awesome in *Moonstruck*. That's one of my favorite movies." Noel laughed when Sunny appeared beside him in the doorway. "I get it, Sunny and Cher!"

Ethan laughed too heartily at the joke and grabbed Noel by the hand. "Dr. Savino, please forgive me for anything I may've said while I had gas. Your hands aren't...well, actually, they are big. It's the long fingers, but I didn't mean to insult them."

"Ethan, quit while you're ahead," Sunny said and smiled when Noel glanced at her. "Nice to see you again, Dr. Savino."

"Call me Noel, please," she said, unsuccessfully trying to pry her hand free of Ethan's grasp. He gazed up at her like an adoring child dressed in a black corset and curly wig. "Is this your Halloween costume?"

"Oh, no, it's just Saturday. Tomorrow, I'll be Audrey Hepburn. Although with your coloring and maybe some brown contacts, you'd make a much better Audrey. What's your dress size?"

Lydia walked onto the porch. "Aw, man, what's he doing?"

Sunny shook her head slowly as she folded her arms. "I think it's a form of hero worship, but you'd better get her quickly, or he's going to try to dress her up."

"Dude, get off her, we have to go."

"I baked a pie, come enjoy it with us later." Ethan squeezed Noel's hand. "Promise you will."

Noel nodded. "Okay, sure."

"I told you it wasn't just the gas that made him that way," Sunny quipped, drawing an ugly glance from Ethan.

"Lydia, if we let the ancients talk, we'll be here all day. Grab an arm," Harper said as she took Noel by the sleeve.

Ethan reluctantly released his hold. "Have fun, girls," he called after the trio as they walked Noel backward down the walk.

"It was good seeing y'all again," Noel called out with her gaze set on Sunny. "I look forward to chatting later."

Sunny waved and went inside with Ethan on her heels. "You went a little ga-ga out there."

"Lady Gaga is a weekday outfit. I'm trying to make up for what happened in her office. Now I have to make a pie."

"I thought you said you already baked one."

"I lied, that's how committed I am to giving you a chance to spend time with her."

Sunny moved to the windows and stared into the backyard with the image of Noel in a pair of worn jeans and gray T-shirt. Her hair was down and unruly. The look was incredibly sexy, especially when she gazed back at Sunny with interest showing clearly in her green eyes. Noel was a huntress, that was made clear by the way she boldly held Sunny's gaze, a slight smile curving her lips. Harper had admitted as much.

Pots and pans banged behind her as Ethan prepared to whip up his pie. "What're you thinking about?"

"Sex."

"The old mind is coming alive! She's old enough to be tamed. This game is as old as time." Ethan opened the freezer and pulled out a bag of fruit, stared at it, and tossed it back in. "You are the one in control. You have what she wants, keep it out of her reach until she gets to know you. That's the problem with women that look like her. Her quarry gives up the fight too easily, and she gets bored."

Sunny turned away from the window. "She's the prey. I won't try to keep her, I only want to play for a while." She held up a hand when Ethan opened his mouth to speak. "I've been going about this all wrong. I've searched for someone to grow old with, but you used to say when the fire in the bedroom dies, it's all laundry and bitching after that. My life is full, I have you and Lydia, work, and all I'm missing is the flame. Noel Savino will give me that, and I'm taking," she said as she walked out of the room.

While Lydia was totally entranced by a Halloween village at the craft store, Harper found Noel looking at the paints. "You can't go out with Lydia's mother. I saw the way you looked at her," Harper whispered.

Noel put a hand to her ear. "Hear that? It's the sound of a new leaf turning over. I'm done with hooking up. I want to do more than mate, I want to date."

"I've heard that before." Harper took a bottle of paint from Noel's hand and tossed it into the basket she carried. "Lydia is the first person I've ever been friends with who really gets me. I like her, I don't feel like a misfit with her. And I don't want you to defile her mother."

"Now you're being insulting," Noel said seriously.

"I'm sorry, but you never have a problem finding women. I don't make good friends easily. I've got frenemies. Lydia is best friend material."

Noel narrowed her eyes. "Fren...what?"

"Frenemies, they call themselves friends, but they'll knife you in the back."

"I'm following now," Noel said with a nod. "Harpy, you're not a misfit."

"Yes, I am. I don't fit in with anyone. Corey's a cheerleader, Mason's the quarterback, and I'm queen of the geeks that want to use me to get to them because they're popular. Lydia doesn't care about any of that."

Noel knew what it felt like to be an outcast. She smiled sadly as she touched Harper's face. "You're only less if you believe it, baby. You are so incredibly special, I wish you could see that."

"In your eyes only. Everyone else sees me as the chunky ugly cousin of gorgeous Corey Savino."

Noel opened her mouth and closed it when Lydia came flying around the corner with something in her hand.

"Check it." She held up a gnarled tree with small plastic pumpkins imprinted with numbers in the packaging. "It's a counter. You count down to Halloween."

"Cool find," Noel said with a smile. "Toss it in the basket."

Noel left the store a hundred eighteen dollars later with buyer's remorse, but the excitement on the girls' faces over such a simple thing made it worthwhile. Noel and Harper had been adding to the village since Harper was nine years old. Mary and David had divorced then, and while Mary coped with the betrayal of a thieving and philandering husband, Noel took Harper under her wing. For them, painting was cathartic, and they bonded during the hours spent together. Noel was thrilled that even though Harper was growing up, she still wanted to work with her on the village.

"Let's get a straw bale for your porch and put some mums and pumpkins on it," Harper suggested as she bounced in her seat.

"Okay, we'll get one for the apartment, too," Noel said.

"No one ever sees it because it's in back of Nana and Pops's house."

"You'll see it, and so will your mom." Noel slowed and made a turn. "We can put it at the bottom of the steps."

Harper shook her head. "It's not home, it's just a temporary place until we can afford something else. No need to dress it up." She turned and smiled at Lydia. "Do y'all decorate for Halloween?"

Lydia shrugged. "We carve a pumpkin. Ethan loves to dress up in case you haven't noticed. Last year, he was Cleopatra. He made Tobi wear a little gold coat, which she shredded in protest."

Noel glanced at Lydia in the rearview. "He's very interesting."

"Mom always says he's her mom and dad rolled into one, and for me, he's like a grandpa." Lydia smiled. "And grandma."

"Are your grandparents…gone?" Harper asked.

"Kind of. They're still alive, but I never met them. Ira and Janice Chase. I refuse to call them my grandparents. Ira ran Ethan off because he's gay, then they did the same to my mom for the same reason." Lydia sighed. "I figure they'd hate me, too, if they knew me. The queer gene is obviously strong in my family." She met Noel's gaze when she glanced in the rearview again. "Are you the only one in yours?"

Noel nodded.

Lydia looked away. "Must be hard. At least I've got Mom and Ethan."

"Coming out was scary because my family is Catholic, and I didn't know how they'd take the news." Noel smiled and glanced at Harper. "I worried for nothing."

Noel's mind started to wander as the girls began to talk about hunting ghosts. She and Harper lived parallel lives, it seemed at times. In her case, Matthew had been the school's star receiver, and Mary was the cheerleader and homecoming queen. Noel began grappling with her sexuality in her freshman year, and it made her feel awkward. But when her sexuality was thrust out in the open by the betrayal of someone she believed was a friend, she truly learned what it meant to be odd girl out.

At the fruit stand, Noel ran into one of her friends, and while she stood talking to her, Lydia and Harper went through a huge pile of pumpkins looking for the right shape and the perfect stem. Lydia watched as Harper picked her way through the pile, a red baseball cap she'd found in Noel's car on her head backward. Her long dark hair hung down beneath it and fanned over her shoulders and back. The T-shirt she wore was long and hit her midthigh; boot-cut jeans hugged her legs and were frayed at her heel because they were too long. She was absolutely gorgeous, and Lydia released a sigh as she stared.

"What's wrong?" Harper said suddenly as she turned.

"It's overwhelming, there's so many," Lydia said and picked up a pumpkin near her feet. "What do you think of this one?"

"It's cute, but it doesn't have much of a stem." Harper moved close. "We should do your porch, too. Noel can fit two straw bales in the trunk of her car, it's huge."

Lydia breathed in Harper's scent and reveled in the closeness. "I don't think I have that much money with me."

Harper grinned. "I do."

Lydia smiled, feeling light-headed with desire coursing through her veins, and watched as Harper resumed her pumpkin hunt. "Hey, I was wondering if you want to stay at my house tonight, watch the horror movie marathon, and eat junk."

"Oh, wow, you had me at junk," Harper said with a laugh. "I have to ask my mom, but she probably won't say no."

"Okay, cool."

Chapter 7

Sunny awoke suddenly when she heard Lydia call to her. She sat up on the sofa as Lydia came bounding into the living room. "I didn't expect you back so early."

"I'm still going to Harper's place, but you need to come to the front porch. Where's Uncle Ethan?"

Sunny rubbed her eyes. "I don't know. I was asleep when you came in," she said and jumped up horrified of what her hair must've looked like. She was about to dart into the bathroom to brush her teeth and do something about her appearance when Lydia dragged Ethan out of the salon.

"Come on, Mom," Lydia said as she caught her by the wrist.

On the porch was a bale of straw set in the corner by the front door, covered in pumpkins, Indian corn, and potted mums of different colors. "Oh, it's so pretty," Ethan exclaimed. "I just love it!"

Harper beamed. "It's a housewarming gift from us and well...Lydia, too."

Noel, who stood at a distance with her hands in her pockets, smiled when Sunny gazed at her. "Thank you all very much," Sunny said with a warm smile.

Ethan rushed over to Noel, gave her a hug, and took her by the arm. "I just put on a pot of coffee, please come in and enjoy. Except for Donovan next door, we don't really know anyone in town, so we don't have such lovely company that often." Ethan gazed up at Noel. "Did you know that my mouth was a hundred percent better by the evening when I saw you?"

"I'm glad to hear that." Noel looked around as Ethan led her through the front door into the kitchen. "You have a beautiful home."

"Thank you. Now you sit here at the table and let me pamper you." Ethan turned to Sunny, who followed. "You sit down, too. I have this."

"I should go freshen up first. I was napping before y'all got here."

Noel's gaze swept over her. "I wish I looked that good when I first wake up."

Sunny backed out of the kitchen with a shy smile. "Thanks, I'll be back in a few."

Ethan motioned for Harper to sit when she tried to help. "Lydia and I can handle the serving, but thank you just the same."

She "accidentally" bumped into Noel as she sat and drew her finger across her neck when Noel glanced at her.

"Where did Cher go?" Noel asked as she returned her attention to Ethan and his kimono.

"That leather corset dress kills me. I can only take it for so long, and I need to get better boots that aren't as clunky. I did have the outfit she wore in the *Turn Back Time* video, but it was way too revealing."

Lydia made a derisive grunt, then covered it with a cough as she poured the coffee. "It's even revealing on the mannequin upstairs. She blushes whenever I go up there."

Noel's eyes glazed over. "Has Sunny ever—" She whirled around to Harper, who had kicked her. "Did your foot slip?" she ground out.

"Did your tongue?" Harper replied just as angrily.

Noel glared at her as she said, "I was going to ask if Sunny ever dresses up."

"A few weeks ago, Ethan turned her into Madonna," Lydia said as she began bringing the coffee cups to the table.

Sunny walked back into the room fresh-faced, her hair and teeth brushed. "Let's not rehash that. Ethan, you sit down and relax. I heard you fussing around in here all afternoon."

Ethan pulled out the chair beside Noel and sat. "What did y'all get into today?"

"A lot of shopping. We hit the craft store and the fruit stand, my car is loaded. Then we stopped for pizza," Noel said.

"Oh, man, that was the best I've ever had," Lydia said with a groan. "It was at that weird pink building on Government Street. Next time we have pizza, we need to get it from there."

"So you've lived here all your life?" Sunny asked as she set a slice of chocolate chip pecan pie in front of Noel.

"My parents are from Long Island, but my siblings and I were all born here," Noel said.

"How'd they end up all the way down here?" Ethan asked.

Harper covered her face and whispered, "Oh, no."

Noel laughed. "I'll give them the short version. After my dad got out of the navy, he was looking for work. A buddy of his told him they were building rigs like crazy off the coast, and he could make more in a couple of months here than in a year in New York. Rich already had a job lined up, and he told Dad that he was sure he could get him one, too. So Dad told Mom that he'd come here and work for a little while, then he'd come home and they could move her out of his parents' house. So Rich and Dad take a bus south in the middle of July. When they arrive, Rich steps off and is hit with a wall of humid heat. He turns to Dad and says, 'No way am I working in this crap.' He gave Dad the contact information for the job, bought a ticket, and got right back on a bus. Dad was a marine engineer in the navy, so they hired him the second he walked in the door. He did make good money, but not what Rich had claimed. Dad kept telling Mom, 'Just a little longer,' and after six months of that, she bought a ticket and came south. They just never left."

Ethan rested his chin in his hand. "That's so romantic. She left her family to be with her love."

"She said it was because she would go to prison for assault if she had to spend one more day with her mother-in-law," Harper added. "And she wanted to learn voodoo, so she could be as big of a pain in great-grandma Vera's ass as she was in hers. The doll is still in the china cabinet at the house, but Pops made her take the pin out of its butt."

Noel smiled at Sunny as she put the rest of the pie plates on the table and noticed the glare in Harper's eyes. She cleared her throat and set her attention on Ethan. "You're not from here, I can tell."

"Cape Girardeau, Missouri, is where we hail from originally. I moved to St. Louis, and when Sunny left home, she stayed with me for a little while, then she went off on her own. When Lydia was born, we moved back in together and have been roommates ever since."

"We've lived in every town along the Mississippi River," Lydia said. "Mom's job keeps us moving, but this is supposed to be our last stop."

"It is our last," Sunny assured. "I started off with a safety contractor that did inspections and training. They moved us all over the place. I thought that ended when I began working for Grant Petrochemical, but they recently moved me here when they expanded their facilities. Harper told us all about the Halloween village you add to each year, I'd like to hear about that."

Noel nodded as she swallowed a bite. "We've been doing it since she was little. I got the idea from my dad. For some unknown reason, someone gave him a case of tongue depressors when I was around five years old. They sat in the garage for a few years, and one December, he came up with the bright idea of making houses out of them. The Savino Christmas Village came into being then," Noel said with a wistful sigh. "I remember sitting at the kitchen table with him for hours gluing and painting and my mother griping that we were getting paint all over the place. We were almost evicted when I glued a placemat to the tabletop."

"Do you still add to that village?" Sunny asked.

Noel made a face. "No. We stored it in the attic, and the heat melted the glue. The next year when Dad brought it down, there was nothing but painted sticks in the bottom. I've got a bunch of pictures to remind me of it, though."

Sunny glanced at Lydia. "We had a Christmas ornament tradition that Ethan started on Lydia's first Christmas. Her favorite toy was a stuffed Dalmatian—"

"Chew toy," Ethan interjected. "The child was like a goat then, she slobbered and gnawed on everything."

Lydia bumped him. "Dude, I'm sure they don't care."

Sunny rolled her eyes and watched the mild shoving match between Ethan and Lydia. "Anyway, whatever she was into that year, we either bought or made an ornament to represent it. The first was a little Dalmatian. Last year, Ethan cut the hair on a troll doll because Lydia cut hers off. Our tree isn't typical."

Ethan jutted his chin proudly. "That's how we like it. We're about as untraditional as a family can get. What're the holidays like with the Savinos?"

"Just as insane as usual, but with a tree," Harper said. "Nana yells at Pops because he builds a huge fire in the fireplace and makes it so hot we can't sit in the living room. He wears shorts year-round and complains that he's cold. Nana cooks nonstop and expects us to eat it all."

Noel held up her fork. "This is absolutely delicious, Ethan. Even my mother, master chef in her own mind, would be impressed."

Ethan patted the back of his left hand with his right. "This is my version of a clap," he said with delight.

Noel noticed the scarring on the back of his hand. "What happened?"

"It was crushed." Ethan touched his forefinger to his thumb. "That's about all the mobility I have in it. A semi failed to stop for a signal light and ended up hitting two vehicles, one of which slammed into my car. I ended up having to get an attorney when a lawyer from the trucking company responsible showed up at my door with a ten thousand-dollar check. My prosthetic eye cost more than that, so of course, I didn't take the deal. I count myself fortunate that I can still use it some. Others were injured a lot worse than I was," he said, gazing at Sunny sadly.

"I'm very sorry," Noel said with sincerity.

"It's getting kind of late," Lydia interjected abruptly. "Should we go paint?"

Ethan frowned. "Oh, no, it's already getting dark. Are we not having horror movie night?"

Noel finished off her last bite of pie and wiped her mouth. "I didn't realize how much time we spent at the fruit stand. Lydia, Sunday is wide open for me. We can get started in the morning and paint all day if you have plans tonight," she said with a glance at Sunny, then turned her attention to Harper. "What've you got planned for tomorrow?"

"Lydia invited me to stay with her tonight and watch movies. We could just both come over in the morning if Mom says I can stay here."

"Why don't you ask her now?" Lydia suggested. "If she says yes, I can take you to get your stuff."

Harper pulled out her phone and began tapping the screen with her thumbs. Noel did the same. "I'll tell her I met the Chases, and I give my approval," Noel said with a grin.

Ethan winked at Sunny. "We're approved, it was my pie."

"No, it was the special bean blend I ground up for the coffee," Sunny countered.

"Both were delicious," Noel said, ending the debate.

Harper pumped her fist. "She says yes!"

Lydia jumped up. "Let's go."

Noel had barely gotten out of her chair when the back door slammed. "Talk about getting dropped like a hot rock."

"They aren't going anywhere fast," Sunny said with a smile. "You have the driveway blocked."

Noel picked up her plate, but Ethan breezed by and took it from her. "I have this, my dear."

"Well, thank you both for the hospitality. I enjoyed the treats and the conversation."

"I'll walk you out," Sunny offered.

Ethan gave Noel a quick hug and hung on to her. "Come for dinner one night. I promise that I'm not buttering you up for free dental work. To be honest, I hate being in your chair."

Noel nodded and smiled. "I'd love to."

Ethan fanned his good hand at Sunny. "Get her number when you walk her out."

"Yes, your excellency, anything else?" Sunny said and bowed low.

"I'll have the list done when you get back inside." Ethan gazed up at Noel. "Thank you for the decorations, I love them."

"I'm glad to hear that. I was worried that maybe we were being too presumptuous."

"No, just very thoughtful." Ethan said with a smile.

"He's adorable," Noel said when she and Sunny stepped outside.

"He is," Sunny said with a sigh. "Ethan's been my rock for a long time. He thinks that I'm taking care of him since he was disabled in the accident, but the truth is, I don't know what I'd do without him."

"I think it's great that you two are so close."

Sunny rubbed her arms to stave off the cool night air. "Yeah…sometimes too close. Especially when he's in the mood to wax up my face."

"My mother lives three doors down from me. The other night, she made me sit in her secret hideout, which is in the hedge, and spy on our neighbors. I understand all about eccentricity," Noel said as she climbed into her car.

"I've been given an order to get your phone number." Sunny leaned against the open door. "We really aren't going to call you for free fishbone removals. I'm pretty sure I can get the job done next time with a mallet and a pair of needle-nosed pliers."

Noel laughed as she fished a pen and a slip of paper from her console. "I'm afraid to ask what the mallet is for."

"It'll work faster than the gas and won't wear off nearly as fast."

Noel laughed as she handed Sunny her number.

Sunny took it and regarded Noel for a moment. "He *is* going to call you."

Noel nodded. "Good. You can call me, too."

A smile spread across Sunny's face. She nodded as she stepped out of the way of Noel's door. "Good night."

As Noel drove out of Sunny's driveway, she grimaced. "Forgive me, Harper."

Chapter 8

"Where have you been and who are these Chase people?" Inez asked when Noel walked through the back door.

"I've been unloading straw and pumpkins outta my car by myself since Harper dumped me to hang out with Lydia." Noel held up a hand. "The Chases are good people. I had coffee with them this afternoon."

Mary, who was seated at the kitchen table, threw up a hand. "See, Mom. You met Lydia, too, and she's a very polite girl. She's a good kid, right, Noel?"

"Yeah, I like her a lot."

Inez still looked suspicious. "What do her parents do?"

"What? You didn't interrogate Lydia when you met her?" Noel grabbed a glass from the cabinet and sat next to Mary at the table where she poured herself some wine.

"Mary wouldn't let me."

"Lydia lives with her mother and uncle in a very nice house a few miles from here. Ethan, the uncle, was disabled in a car accident, so they take care of each other. Sunny works for some petrochemical company."

"What about the father?" Inez pressed.

Noel shrugged. "I have no idea."

Inez threw up a hand. "What do you know?"

"All three of them are gay."

Mary blinked rapidly. "So Lydia is a lesbian."

Noel nodded slowly. "And she's Harper's friend."

"Hey, I'm not being a homophobe. I was just a little surprised there for a second," Mary said defensively.

Inez came around the kitchen counter. "Noel, did Harper jump on the fence?"

"What? No. It's 'jump the fence,' by the way."

"You would know. You would spot the signs before we did," Inez said as her eyes bore into Noel's.

"I would, and I also believe that Harper would come to me if her sexuality was in question. So far, all I see are two girls with a lot in common, and they're having fun."

"All right. Okay," Mary said with a nod and downed her glass of wine.

Inez pursed her lips as she continued to stare at Noel and nodded. "So the mom is gay, she single?"

"Harper says yes."

"She a cat?" Inez asked with a slight smile.

"I see she's given you that speech, too." Mary refilled her wineglass and added more to Noel's, though she had not had any yet. "I'm supposed to look for a dog that's neutered."

"You two make fun, but it's true," Inez said as she took a seat at the table. "Listen to your momma."

Joe shuffled into the kitchen in his pajamas. "Inez, where's the amaretto?"

Inez propped her chin in her hand and held up a finger as she gazed at her girls. "It's where we keep it."

Joe walked over to the cabinet beside the pantry, opened the door, and stared. "I don't see it."

"Did you think it was gonna jump out and hug your neck? Move things around!" Inez spat out.

"I wanna make an amaretto freeze. How do I do that? Do I use the blender?"

"I'll make it for you, Daddy," Mary said as she jumped up.

Inez winked at Noel, and they watched as Mary quickly whipped up Joe's drink. By the time she finished, Joe was already back in his chair in the living room. Mary wrapped the glass in a paper towel and took it to him.

"You're a dog," Inez said when Mary rejoined them at the table. "The dog is eager to serve and please." She shook a finger at Mary. "Find you a man dog, and he'll take care of you like you take care of him."

"I think you're wrong about Dad being a dog," Noel said with a smirk. "He just manipulated Mary into making him a drink, that's so cat."

Inez nodded with a look of resignation. "He may be a cog."

Ethan paused the movie and looked like he was having a seizure as he flopped around on the sofa. "I hate it when something comes out from under the bed!"

Harper laughed at his antics. Normally, she would've been equally as disturbed by the scene that they'd just watched, but she was nestled beneath a blanket between Lydia and Sunny. She felt safe, and the jokes made throughout the movie lessened the fear factor.

"Dude, be still, you're knocking the popcorn out of the bowl," Lydia said as she passed it to Harper.

Ethan snuggled closer to Lydia. "I can't help it, things beside and underneath the bed is my horror movie Achilles heel. Sunny, expect company tonight."

"Oh, yippee," she said drolly.

Ethan leaned forward and caught Harper's eye. "You said Noel watches horror movies?"

Harper nodded. "She won't watch anything slasher, though. While we're painting the add-ons to the village, we watch *Hocus Pocus* and *Lady in White* because that's what we watched when we first began."

"She's big on tradition, isn't she?" Sunny said as she grabbed a handful of popcorn.

"Oh, yeah," Harper said with a laugh. "My nana has wanted a fake Christmas tree for years, but Noel throws a fit because they've always had a live tree, and she thinks that shouldn't change."

Sunny smiled. "Your family seems to be very close."

"Nana likes it that way. We all live in the same neighborhood, and every Sunday, we get together for dinner," Harper said and rolled her eyes. "It's so loud."

Ethan blew out a breath. "I think I'm ready to resume the movie now. Is everyone else?"

"Yeah, titty baby." Lydia laughed when Ethan glared at her. "Dude, stop trying to hold my hand."

Moonlight shined through the big windows of the living room and illuminated the sofa where Harper lay beneath a blanket. Lydia watched her as she toyed with a strand of her hair. "What're you thinking about?" Lydia whispered.

"I like your family," Harper said softly. "I'm glad y'all moved here."

"Me too. Are you going to college?"

"Mom wants me to go to LSU because it's close to home. She and Nana want me to study something in the medical field." Harper sighed. "I don't know what I want to do."

"I'm going to school here, too. Let's get an apartment together."

"They make you stay in the dorms freshman year unless you're local and you live with your parents, but we could after our first year."

"I want a Ping-Pong table."

Harper laughed softly. "That'd be fun. We'd live off popcorn and pizza and watch creepy movies that scare the shit outta us."

"We'll have beanbag chairs and boxes for furniture, maybe an old couch we find at a secondhand store." Lydia sighed at the notion. "Broadway posters all over the walls."

"I'm good with everything but the couch. You don't know what may be living inside of it. People screw on those things all the time. The cushions are probably covered in spooge."

Lydia gagged and laughed. "You ruined my dream."

"I'm so not sorry about that. It'll be my job to protect you from biohazards."

"What will be my job?"

Harper was quiet for a moment, her voice was heavy with sleepiness when she said, "You'll have to make me laugh."

"Always," Lydia whispered.

Noel sat straight up in bed when she heard what sounded like the shrill sound her alarm made just before she punched in the code to switch it off. Thinking that she'd been dreaming, she began to lie back down when something clanked in her kitchen. She got up and grabbed her bat from the closet just to be on the safe side and crept down the hall.

"Momma! The sun ain't even up, what're you doing?"

"Making coffee." Inez stared at the one-cup maker perplexed. "How the hell do you work this thing? Why don't you have a normal pot like everyone else?"

Noel still had the bat slung over her shoulder as she walked over to where Inez stood. "Is someone dead or in the hospital?"

"No, I woulda called you if that was the case."

Noel's brow shot skyward, and her voice sounded whiny as she said, "Then why on earth are you here at this time of the morning on a weekend?"

"I was thinking." Inez huffed and threw up a hand. "Noel, make me some coffee, I can't figure this thing out. None of that flavored shit, just give me the real stuff."

Noel grabbed one of the single-serve packs and tossed it into the brewer. "Couldn't you have waited to tell me what you were thinking about after the sun came up?"

"I wanted to give you time to invite Lydia's mom and uncle to eat with us today. Matt and the kids are going with Lauren to some function at her parents' place." Inez shrugged. "We have room, and we should invite them because they had you over for coffee."

Noel narrowed her eyes. "You just want to be nosy and get into their business."

Inez nodded. "Yeah. I got something else on my mind, too. Harper hasn't gone out with a boy since her sophomore year. You find that strange?"

"She went to prom last year with Monroe Tatum."

"As friends. Now she's got a close friend that's a lesbian."

"That means she has an open nonjudgmental mind, not necessarily that she's gay." Noel took a cup from the cabinet and filled it with coffee. "You want liquid creamer or the powdered stuff?" she asked as she set the coffeemaker to brew another cup.

Inez tasted the coffee and smacked her lips. "Neither, this ain't half bad. I couldn't sleep last night thinking about Harper. You know, she's not anything like Corey. I keep telling Matt to put that girl of his on birth control, or he's gonna be a grandfather before she gets outta high school. Harper, she's never looked at a boy the way Corey does." She slowly lowered the cup to the counter. "I don't know if I can watch another one of my babies go through this. You were her age when you came home from school crying, your heart broken because you confided in a friend that let you down. The torment you endured when word got out broke my heart."

"That won't happen again. You're probably worrying over nothing."

Inez licked her lips. "So what I need to know is if you're in denial about Harper, or if you really don't see anything in her."

"Momma, things are different now."

"That's not what I asked."

Noel released a sigh. "Sometimes, I think I sense it in her, but I could be wrong. That's why I haven't shared my suspicions. Besides, we can't compare Harper to Corey. They are polar opposites when it comes to personality. Corey moves with the herd, Harper does her own thing."

Inez set her hand atop Noel's. "If she comes to you about this, you come to me. Promise me that."

"I will, unless she swears me to secrecy."

"Call those people, invite them to come eat. If Harper is gonna spend time with them, we should know them."

"Okay," Noel said with a nod.

Inez grabbed Noel and pulled her into a hug. "You know I'm proud of you."

Noel smiled. "I do."

"And I love you," Inez said as she pulled back and patted Noel's cheek.

"I loved you before you woke me up."

"Smartass. You get that from your father. I'm going to check my roast." Inez picked up her coffee cup. "I'm taking this with me. Call the people."

"I love you, too, Mom," Noel said with a laugh.

"Yeah, you do."

Noel folded her arms and watched her tough-talking little tiger of a mother stroll down her driveway. Inez was just as protective over Harper as she was, and that was why Noel couldn't fully divulge her intuition about Harper. Noel had noticed long ago that all of Harper's heroes were women, and she had a special affinity for her female teachers. Inez was right, Harper appeared to view boys as peers, not something desirous. Of course, none of this meant that Harper was gay, but Noel had been the same way when she was growing up.

"Does she do that every morning?" Harper asked as she stared through the window at Sunny, who sat in the lotus position on a mat in the middle of the patio.

"Just on the weekends." Lydia shook her head. "I can't meditate. I tried, but when I sit that still, I fall asleep."

"Then you have achieved inner peace," Harper said with a laugh and looked at her phone when it vibrated. She started to ignore Noel's text asking for Sunny's number, but the request began to burr under her skin. Just the day before, she'd asked Noel to leave Sunny alone. She apparently was being ignored. *Why????* Harper typed back with a frown.

Because your nosy Nana woke me up at dawn and demanded that I invite them to dinner. U know she won't stop until she gets what she wants.

Harper knew this to be true and sighed, but she still didn't want Noel having Sunny's number. So she made a call. "Sunny's outside meditating. When she's done, I'll call you and you can talk to her then."

"Look at you trying to build your own little buffer zone."

"Mm-hmm," Harper said as she watched Lydia mix up two chocolate milks.

"I'm just following orders."

Harper turned when Sunny walked in the back door carrying her mat. "Ms. Sunny, Noel would like to talk to you," she said and held out her phone.

Sunny took it with a smile. "Good morning."

"Same to you. I hate to hit you with a question first thing, but I'm under orders to do so, and I know you understand how that is."

"It's nice to know that someone shares my plight," Sunny replied with a laugh. "What's up?"

"Well," Noel began with a sigh. "My mother showed up very early this morning insisting that I invite you and your family to eat with us today. I'd love to have y'all join us, but I must warn you that you may need therapy after the encounter. We Savinos are loud, and my mother's nosy. Feel free to decline if you're breaking out into hives just thinking about it."

"Since you put it that way, I don't suppose I can resist. I hope it won't offend you or your mother, but Ethan will more than likely not join us. He still has big phobias about being in a car. I would've never gotten him to your office if he had not been in pain."

"Give him a heads-up. Mom will send him a huge plate. We get together at three, it's a late lunch/early dinner kind of thing. Come earlier, though, if you'd like to see the village. Harper will give you the address and directions."

"What can I bring—dessert, wine, bread?"

"Trust me, we have it all. Just bring you and your appetite."

"I'm going to ignore you on that," Sunny said with a smile. "But I'll see you soon."

When the call ended, Sunny handed the phone back to Harper. "I'm going to need the address to Noel's house."

Lydia was sporting a chocolate milk mustache when she asked, "For what?"

"Harper's grandmother invited us to have dinner with them today, and if you don't clean your mouth before Ethan sees it, he'll try to wax your lip."

Harper held up both hands in defense. "Please promise you won't judge me after meeting my family. They're crazy, but it's a lovable crazy after you get used to them."

Ethan walked into the kitchen at that moment wearing a royal blue evening gown that was two sizes too small. "I'm so brokenhearted," he cried. "My girlish figure has fled and left me with the body of an old man! He woke up in my bed bloated and puffy." He stamped his foot. "Someone wrap me in seaweed immediately."

Lydia smiled at Harper wryly. "We know crazy."

Chapter 9

Ethan walked briskly down the hall with a pink barbell in one hand and another duct taped to his left. He stopped and backed up when he noticed clothing flying out of Sunny's closet. "Please tell me that's you and this house isn't possessed."

Sunny released a low growl and said in a creepy voice, "Your closet is next."

"Not funny, you know it's too early in the day for demons. Is this fall cleaning?"

"Noel's mother invited us to have lunch with them today. They don't live far from here, would you consider joining me?"

Ethan took a seat on Sunny's bed. "No, but please thank her for me. What're you looking for?"

"Something that doesn't make me look bloated or old or sloppy."

"Jeans, the red, white, and indigo blue plaid button-down shirt with a white cami underneath, and those brown boots you have. It's casual sexy."

Sunny pulled the shirt Ethan mentioned from her closet and stared at it. "That's what I want."

"What are you going to do with your face?"

Sunny shrugged as she looked through her jeans. "I guess I'll wear that, too."

"You're such a shit. I want to do a facial, and maybe put on a light foundation with just a touch of mascara."

Sunny spun and tossed a pair of jeans onto the bed. "Will you do my hands?"

Ethan nodded as he got up. "I'll go warm the wax. You shower and come let me make you prettier," he said excitedly and started to dash from the room. He turned and held up the hand taped to the barbell. "Free me, please."

Ethan had slipped into his favorite black cocktail dress and a blond wig. Sunny shook her head as she walked into his salon. "You're going to get wax or something else on that, then you're going to be distraught."

"I already am. I'd planned a whole day around that royal blue gown. I need to stop gorging myself on junk, but then, I'm not happy unless I'm gorged."

All the things he planned to use for the facial were set on a tray next to a chair that reclined. Soft music played in his salon, and he'd lit candles to induce relaxation. He gestured to a chair and wrapped Sunny's hair in a towel when she sat.

"You must want to impress if you're willing to submit to this." Ethan covered Sunny's eyes and began cleansing her skin.

"I'm meeting new people, first impressions, you know."

Ethan smacked his lips. "You are such a liar. This is all about Noel."

"It has everything to do with her. I'm in seduction mode."

Ethan released a sigh. "I still think you're going about this the wrong way. Like I told you, she's at the taming age. With a little patience and care, you could turn her around."

"I'm the one that needs to change. She and I aren't all that different, we don't keep women. I'm tired of getting my hopes up about meeting the right one. Frankly, I think Noel has the right idea by keeping things strictly sexual. I don't know why I didn't see this before."

"Take it from someone who had the same philosophy, the rush fades and you find yourself back in the same place longing for something substantial." Ethan tapped Sunny in the forehead. "Don't lick."

"My lips are dry."

Ethan walked across the room and grabbed a tube of balm. "You're breathing through your mouth a lot, which means you're nervous," he said as he returned and smeared her lips with it.

"I am, this is new territory."

"Maybe it's more than that. Despite her reputation for being a womanizer, I sense a sweet soul. She may've been hurt, too, and she's hiding behind the player disguise."

"I don't want to analyze this, I just want to do it," Sunny said impatiently.

Ethan nodded as he gently exfoliated Sunny's skin. "Sure you do, but if you were totally comfortable with your decision, you wouldn't be this edgy. Tamara was your first real love, the one that sets the standard for all after that. You can't expect every woman you meet to match that level of intensity. Honestly, I think you're afraid that you'll find and lose—"

"Don't lecture me about fear, Ethan," Sunny snapped. "You barely leave this house unless you're forced." She exhaled heavily when he stopped scrubbing at her face and snatched off the eye covers. "I'm sorry. I have no right to judge or minimize what you must feel."

"I'm not judging you, either." Ethan smiled sadly. "I just don't want you to end up like me. No one wants an old banged-up queen." He took the eye covers from her and replaced them. "Don't feel sorry for me, I had my share of fun. Since I've gone through manopause, my desires aren't the same. I'd skip sex any day just to have someone to hold. I used to gripe and complain about having to put up with someone else's wants, but I'd give my left hand to do that now."

Sunny raised one eye patch and stared at Ethan. He grinned. "Well, you don't think I'd give up the only good hand I've got."

He covered Sunny's face with a heavy cream mask and picked up his exfoliating brush and went to work on her hands. "How are you going to tell Noel that you only want sex from her?"

"I don't know, I was hoping maybe you'd give me advice. I mean, I can't just pull her aside and say, I want to get naked with you for a few hours, then go my merry way without restrictions, or…can I?"

"You have got to take better care of your hands, or they're going to look ninety when you're only forty-five. Moisturize more often, for Pete's sake."

"I think that's going to be a moot point if you scrub all the meat off my hand." Sunny resisted the urge to chew at her lip. "What if she rejects me?"

"Now that's what I'd call moot. I saw the lingering glances and the way she smiled at you." Ethan laughed. "Oh, yes, she's interested. Do you want to know what I found in my favorite Jimmy Choo boots this morning?"

It was a minute or two before Sunny replied, "Jimmy?"

"Cat shit. I told her that I was going to enlist your help with cutting her nails today, and she launched a pre-emptive strike. After she finished with the boots, she pissed on my Lana Turner wig."

Sunny's mask was ruined. The cream had bunched into the crevices around her mouth and in her forehead when she laughed. Ethan grinned as he smoothed it back out. "I thought levity might help with your nerves. I'm sure the opportunity will present itself while you're chatting with Noel. She'll probably ask you out, then you simply say you're not interested in commitments, just a good time. She'll understand exactly what that means."

"Thanks."

"Welcome," Ethan said with a frown, feeling that Sunny was settling for far less than she deserved. "Try to keep your face expressionless and go set your hands in the wax."

Sunny got up when Ethan removed the eye covers and walked over to the vat of warm pink goo. "I like this part. My hands feel like velvet when the wax is pulled away."

"It's the emollients. The waxy mixture makes a glove that helps your skin absorb the vitamins."

"Hey, have you ever stuck your face into this stuff?"

Ethan walked over to his nail station and began to rearrange it. "I'm sure someone already has, and if it had worked, they'd be selling face kits. The probable truth is that someone out there has a hairline that hasn't receded naturally because it was ripped out by the damn roots. And what did remain they spent hours picking pieces of wax from it. The product is called Silk Hands for a reason, it's just for hands."

Sunny stared at him for a moment. "You stuck your face in this, didn't you?"

"Twice." He sighed. "You were out of town both times, so I had a chance to repair some of the damage. That's why I straightened my hair and wore it combed forward for a while."

Sunny laughed. "Hey, at least you didn't stick your—" Her face went blank when Ethan began furiously arranging his nail polishes.

"Don't make that face," he screeched when he saw Sunny in one of the large mirrors. "You've ruined your mask and gotten wax all over my floor."

"I *cannot* believe you allowed me to stick my hands in there without disclosing that!"

Ethan picked a piece of lint off his dress and casually stated, "Oh, hey, I stuck my dick in the wax."

Sunny's nostrils flared, and when she began speaking again, she sounded like she had inhaled helium. "You let me, and more importantly my baby, put our hands in something you had sex with?"

"Oh, gross," Ethan said with a flick of his hand. "I had the heat on the lowest setting, but when my doodle just barely touched that stuff, it took off and hid. I nearly had to stick a rubber snake up my ass to scare it back out. If it makes you feel better, I changed the mixture after that unfortunate encounter. Now don't you feel silly for making a mess?"

"You stuck your pecker in a vat of hot wax and you're asking me if I feel stupid?"

"Put your hands back in," Ethan said with exasperation.

Sunny stared at him for a moment. "You promise—"

"I've changed it twice since then," Ethan snapped.

Sunny returned her hands to the wax and watched as Ethan cleaned up the mess. "Did it soften your face?"

"It tore off my eyelashes."

"I like this," Lydia said, sounding surprised at her own admission. She turned the plaster house she had sitting on her fist and began to dab it with paint. "They make new ones every year?"

"Yep, and we get them all," Noel said as she very carefully painted a jack-o'-lantern on the porch of the one she was working on. "Year before last, they came out with the haunted hotel, that's my favorite."

"I found it, but she stole it." Harper shot Noel a disdainful look. "But that's okay because I also found the mortuary, and I think it's the coolest piece we have."

Noel scrunched up her face. "It doesn't have the ghosts hanging out the windows like the hotel."

Lydia grinned at the bantering two. "Maybe when Mom sees these, she will want to do a village. I know Ethan would, he likes crafts. Mom's lucky if she can paint her toenails."

"You can paint with us anytime you want to," Noel said with a smile. She dropped her brush into a cup of water when they heard a knock on the door and got up.

Lydia watched Noel walk away and whispered, "I feel kinda guilty that we didn't tell her she had paint on her nose."

Harper's laugh was evil. "I don't."

"Hey, seriously, this is fun, thanks for letting me hang with y'all."

Harper gazed at Lydia with a warm smile. "Having you here makes it more fun. I hope you'll do it with us from now on."

Sunny was admiring Noel's handiwork with the straw bale when the door opened. Noel greeted her wearing a white apron with plenty of paint smudges on it. "You really get into your crafts, don't you?" Sunny said with a grin.

Noel jutted her chin. "I suffer for my art." She laughed and gestured toward the door. "Please come in, and feast your eyes upon the most awesome Halloween village ever."

Sunny stepped inside the older wood-framed house; it smelled of the pumpkin spice put off by the burning candles on the coffee table. It had been pushed into a corner to make room for the craft table where Lydia and Harper sat. Another table on the opposite side of the room held the famed village.

"Hey, girls, how's it going?" Sunny asked as she walked over to them.

"No pressure, but I'm gonna die if we don't start making one of these for our place." Lydia held up the house she was working on. "Is this cool or what?"

"It is," Sunny said with a nod. "Maybe we can start one for Christmas this year."

"She still has to come paint with us," Harper added. "She's been included in the tradition now."

"Would you like some coffee or something to drink?" Noel asked. "I suggest a glass of wine to steel your nerves for what's ahead."

Sunny laughed. "You and Harper are very sweet, I can't imagine the rest of your family is any different."

Noel held up a finger. "You definitely need wine. Don't look at the village without me," she said as she went into the kitchen.

"Don't tell her about the paint on her nose," Harper whispered.

"Okay." Sunny grinned as she admired the houses and buildings they were painting. "This really is cool. I don't know if I have the skill to make them look as nice."

"It's easy. If you screw up, you just repaint when it's dry," Harper said. "I'm sure Noel has an old shirt I can wear and you can have my apron."

"Oh...no. I'll just watch."

"Don't worry, when she gets a good look at the village, she's gonna want to pick up a brush," Noel said as she returned with the wine and handed it to Sunny. She put a hand on Sunny's lower back and led her over to the display.

The touch caused warmth to spread over Sunny, and she hoped it didn't show on her face. She knew Noel was watching her as she gazed at the village that contained houses, businesses, and even a graveyard. She chuckled at a truck with a werewolf at the wheel. Frankenstein, Dracula and of course, the Wolfman were represented, along with a crew of witches, skeletons, black cats, and every macabre creature associated with Halloween.

"This is really impressive," Sunny said as she took a closer look at the small town.

"Don't look too closely at my earlier work. I sucked," Harper said. "Would you talk Nostalgic Noel into letting me repaint them?"

"No, never." Noel pointed at the houses that were oddly colored and had a lot of mistakes. "I think they're precious just the way they are."

Sunny looked over her shoulder at Harper with an apologetic smile. "Sorry, honey, but I have to agree with her."

Noel moved her hand over Sunny's back. "You should join us. You can start off with something small, and it can be the first piece for the village you'll create with Lydia."

Sunny realized that she would agree to just about anything if Noel kept touching her. "Okay, count me in."

"Take my apron." Noel shrugged out of it and carefully slipped the neck loop over Sunny's head, gazing for a long time at her face. "You're very pretty," she said, sounding as though the words slipped past her lips unconsciously. Harper began to cough and broke the spell. Noel smiled. "Come sit down."

Noel led Sunny to the table and had her sit in her chair. "All right, you have your pick of all the pieces here."

Sunny chose a jack-o'-lantern with a ghost coming out of the top of it. "I probably won't mess this up too badly."

"You'll do fine," Harper assured. "So much better than..." She looked at Noel. "What was the woman's name that tried to make Christmas ornaments and burned her leg with the hot glue?"

Noel narrowed her eyes at Harper aware that she was trying to make her look bad. "Glynn."

"No, that's not the one. It was Christa or Crystal, something like that." Harper shrugged. "There's been so many, I can't keep up."

Sunny gazed at Bette Midler's face covered in garish makeup with bucked teeth protruding from her mouth frozen on the TV screen. "Why...does she look like that?"

"She's about to sing *I Put a Spell on You*. It's one of my favorite scenes in the movie," Noel said. "I paused it because we were all talking. I was about to tell the story about the time Harper drank a whole bottle of magnesium citrate she found in my mother's medicine cabinet. She thought it was grape soda." Noel felt a strong sense of satisfaction when Harper's jaw sagged. "I'll save that one for some other time, though."

Sunny picked up a brush, dabbed it into the orange on Noel's palette, and began to paint. "Lydia, this reminds me of the time you and I found that pumpkin patch. Do you remember that?"

"Vaguely, pumpkins went on for miles or at least it seemed like it did, and there was a pumpkin cannon."

"We used to go on day adventures. Ethan would pack us a lunch, and we'd just drive. One time, we found a goat farm, where they let you hold the baby goats. We spent a whole day there playing with them." Sunny's smile was wistful when she said, "We don't do it much anymore because *someone* is growing up."

Lydia shrugged. "I have to do it sometime."

"They do grow fast. It seems like only yesterday that I was having to remind Harper not to eat the paint...then again, that could've been just yesterday." Noel deftly avoided a swat from Harper's brush.

"Are you planning to go to LSU?" Sunny asked Harper.

"Mom says I am. She's planned my courses all through high school for nursing and has already submitted my application to LSU, so I guess that's where I'm going."

Sunny glanced at her painting. "You definitely don't sound excited about that."

"I don't really know what I want to do, so I'm just rolling with the tide."

"Dental school, you want to go to dental school," Noel whispered repeatedly.

"I never went to college," Sunny admitted. "I wanted to be an anthropologist and travel the world studying human cultures, but my dad said it would be a useless degree unless I wanted to teach. He basically demanded that I take accounting, which he deemed useful."

"So you just didn't go?" Harper asked.

"My mother found love letters I'd exchanged with a girl I was crazy about the summer after I graduated high school. That sort of changed my life course. I went to live with Ethan after that, and I was so angry and rebellious that I didn't go back to school. That was a decision I regret making. I have a good job, but it has taken me years to get to a place where others have walked into with a degree under their belt. Just being on campus and seeing all it has to offer may give you a few ideas while you take your prerequisite courses."

"Like veterinary school," Lydia said with a nudge. "Tobi inspires me. I want to understand why she only wants to lick my face when I sleep."

Sunny frowned as she took the package of flowers from her car. "I thought since it was kind of cool outside these would keep better," she said as she pulled a wilted flower from the bunch.

"They're still very pretty, Mom will love them. You really didn't have to do that, though," Noel said as she watched Lydia and Harper go on ahead of them.

"I know you said that, but I wanted to show my appreciation." Sunny closed her car door and fell in step with Noel as they strolled the sidewalk. "Your family has no problem with your sexuality?"

"When I was forced out of the closet by my best friend in high school, it got kind of ugly. People that I thought were friends turned against me quickly, and those that didn't like me had new ammunition. I didn't tell my folks at first, but one day, I got into a fight, and I had no choice but to admit the truth to my mother. Mom never had a chance to really sit back and think about it, she went immediately into fight mode, and as the queen, the whole family followed suit. They descended on my school like a swarm of angry bees. And now you're about to step into the hive," Noel said with a smile as they walked up on the porch of her parents' home.

Sunny was almost fearful of being stung as she stepped inside and found the Savinos ready to greet her. From the way Noel talked about her mother, Sunny expected to be met with something larger than life. Instead, she gazed at a tiny waif with a head of curly black and silver hair. She had on a little pair of jeans that were probably bought in the children's department and a Saints sweatshirt with a dish towel slung over one shoulder. Her green eyes cut through Sunny like two lasers, and Sunny knew she was being thoroughly inspected.

"I'm Inez, welcome to our home," she said as she took Sunny's hand and squeezed it firmly. "This is my husband, Joe. Excuse him, he doesn't know how to put on pants."

Joe was tall and thin, but his belly poked out beneath his Saints T-shirt, and he had on a pair of green silky basketball shorts and loafers on his feet. He pumped Sunny's hand furiously. "Great to meet you, we love Lydia, she's a great kid."

"Thank you, it's a pleasure to meet you both," Sunny said with a smile.

Inez grabbed a woman who looked very much like Noel except she was much shorter. "This is my Mary, Noel's big sister and Harper's mother."

Mary's handshake was firm but gentle and lingered as she said, "It's so nice to meet you, Sunny. You and Lydia look so much alike."

"I was just thinking the same about you and Noel," Sunny said as she looked at both of them.

"Their momma knows how to lay on a gene. Apparently, you do, too," Joe said. "But the girls have my charming personality."

Inez elbowed him in the hip. "Thank God it's not your sense of style. Sunny, you come on into the kitchen with us girls and leave Fido to his football."

"I thought we were gonna eat now," Joe complained.

"We eat when I say we eat," Inez barked.

Noel grinned. "When she offers you wine, just say yes. I'll drive you home if you have too much."

Inez grabbed a bottle of wine and glass when they walked into her kitchen. "Noel tells me that Ethan is afraid of the car."

"Momma." Noel shook her head.

Inez squinted. "You got paint on your nose," she said as she licked her thumb. "Come here."

"I'll get a paper towel, thank you. I'm not four." Noel's gaze was hard when it fell on Harper. "Thanks for not mentioning the paint, Harpy."

Inez waved the bottle. "Sunny, have a glass of vino?"

"Yes, thank you," Sunny replied. "Ethan had a serious car accident a few years ago, so it's hard to get him to ride in a car for even a short distance. He sends his regards and gratitude for the invitation nonetheless."

Inez set the glass in front of Sunny. "I'm gonna make him a plate for you to take home."

"He'll appreciate not having to cook for a change." Sunny looked around at the small kitchen and adjoining dining room and said, "Inez, you have a lovely, warm-feeling home."

"Thanks, but Harper tells me it looks like chopped liver compared to yours."

"I never said anything about liver." Harper shook her head and rolled her eyes.

"Joe, you turn that TV down, or I swear I'm coming in there," Inez yelled, and the volume immediately lowered. She turned her attention to Noel. "You just missed Greg and DeVito."

"Oh, Momma, please," Mary said with a pained expression. "Her name is Rhonda, and she's a very sweet woman."

"She's Danny DeVito in drag," Inez countered.

Noel winced and hoped that Sunny didn't take offense, but she jumped right into the fray with both feet. "You want to see drag, you should come to my house. Right now, Ethan is Audrey Hepburn, and he's wearing a gown similar to one she wore in *Breakfast at Tiffany's*. He loves to order stuff off the net and dress like the classic actresses in the glamour days. He's changed three times already today."

"Does he do Ava Gardner?" Inez shook a finger. "Now that was a beautiful woman. I wanted to be her when I was younger."

"Her, very early Bette Davis, of course Liz Taylor, Grace Kelly, and he buys replica gowns from famous movies. If he can't find them, he will order something close and send them to a friend to be altered." Sunny shrugged. "It's a hobby, and it makes him happy."

Sunny blended in with ease and answered every question Inez threw at her about where she'd lived, what she did for a living, and how she and Ethan came to live with each other.

Inez smiled, and Noel knew she was impressed. "Loyalty in family is important. He takes care of you, and you do the same. I taught my kids that, so when Joe and I are gone, they'll take care of each other."

Mary patted Noel's cheek. "Poor baby, you're gonna be stuck pushing me around in a wheelchair and looking for Matt's false teeth."

"That's what you have kids for. Leave it to me, and I'll run over Matt's teeth with your chair and stuff you in a closet."

A buzzer went off, and Inez shouted again. "Joe, get in here and take the roast out, slice it up, then we eat."

"I've already starved to death, you're talking to my ghost."

"Joe, you do the honor of the blessing," Inez said as everyone took a seat at the table.

"Dear God, we thank you for this food and the company. Bless Brees's knees. Amen."

"Join hands for the oath." Inez had Sunny seated to her right, displacing Noel. She took her hand. "We started this when Noel came out," she explained quickly. "All right, here we go...At this table, we are all equal. No one here is less, difference is a blessing. We love and support each other, and we'll do the same as our family grows bigger. The whole world can fall apart around us, but we will always stand together because we are the Savinos."

Sunny and Lydia raised their glasses in toast along with everyone else.

"I should've warned you about that," Noel said apologetically.

Sunny was taken aback, unable to imagine her own flesh and blood back home participating in such a gesture. "I'm truly amazed and touched." She looked around the table. "That's an awesome thing to do as a family."

"While we're keeping with tradition, you may as well go ahead and tell the bread story," Harper said drolly.

Inez cleared her throat. "It was a beautiful fall day just like this one in Long Island…"

Chapter 10

Harper and Lydia were just silhouettes with the security light behind them as they sat in Harper's old treehouse. Their legs dangled over the sides of the plain platform ten feet off the ground. Harper stared at the flickering flames in the fire pit on the patio where Noel and Sunny sat talking. "I want to ask you something very personal."

"I've never been with a guy."

"How'd you—" Harper sighed. "You get asked that a lot. I'm sorry."

"Yep, and when I say no, they ask, 'How do you know you're really gay then?'"

Harper smiled. "And then you say, 'How do you know you're really straight if you haven't slept with a member of the same sex?'"

"No, my response is, 'I don't have to take a bite of shit to know I don't like it.'"

"Oh, that's gross, but so much more impactful," Harper said with a laugh.

"I don't have anything against guys. If I was ever going to be with a guy, it would've been Pokey, my best friend in Little Rock. He's so good-looking, he's almost pretty. Perfect hair, his face never breaks out, that makes me hate him a little bit, and he's got these full lips that are always red. We had everything in common, the way we thought about things was the same. If he had been a girl, I would've been totally in love with him." Lydia shook her head and pulled a knee to her chest. "I thought about...you know, trying him. We kissed once. Those lips were nice to look at, but I didn't like them on mine. I felt—it felt wrong, like I was doing something unnatural."

"Have you slept with a girl?"

Lydia shrugged. "Kinda?"

"How do you *kinda* have sex?"

"We did some things, not everything," Lydia said as she toyed with a string on one of her bracelets. "I spent the night at her house, and I was just so freaked out thinking her mother might walk into her room."

"Was she your girlfriend?"

"No. Just someone who wanted to see what it was like. We never did anything else after that." Lydia pulled her other foot onto the platform and wrapped her arms around her legs. "Have you done it?"

"Yeah, only once. It was on my list of things to do," Harper confessed nonchalantly. "We weren't together or anything, he took me to prom. It was okay. I might've been more into it if I'd cared about him, but I didn't. I almost changed my mind when he tried to put the rubber on the wrong way, and it shot into the ceiling fan. I kinda took that as an omen, but he had another one."

Lydia's laugh rumbled out of her chest. "Did you find the shit that hit the fan?"

"We had to. If his mom woulda found that in the game room, she'd have killed him. It was behind the air hockey table with dust bunnies stuck to it." Lydia's laughter was infectious, and Harper joined her. "Could you see that stuck to their dog? One night, Monroe's family is all sitting at the kitchen table, and Noodle runs in with it on his snout. If it were me, I'd claim I was teaching him to practice safe sniffing."

"Listen to them, they're cackling like two hens," Noel said with a chuckle. "They really bonded quickly."

"I'm glad because I think Harper is an awesome kid."

"Me too," Noel said with a warm smile. "I think the same of Lydia."

"Your mom isn't anything like you made her out to be," Sunny said as she watched the girls.

Noel wagged a finger and laughed. "Oh, you have no idea. You didn't meet the real Inez Savino tonight, but if you come to dinner again, you will."

"Remember, I've got Ethan, nothing shocks me."

"My mother throws rotten peaches at cars that she thinks travel too fast down our street. I've been hit twice, and I was doing the speed limit."

"Ethan steals my bras."

Noel bit her bottom lip and wrinkled her nose. "You may have me beat."

"He's probably got one on right now and his Madonna wig lip syncing to *Like a Virgin* into the broom handle. I find him doing that all the time when I come home unexpected. The poor cat just stares at him with fascination."

"I'd like to see that," Noel said with a grin.

Sunny held her gaze. "My bra or Ethan performing in front of a one-cat audience?"

Noel didn't miss the innuendo. "Both."

"I can make those arrangements," Sunny said softly.

"Harper has forbidden me to ask you out."

Sunny's brow rose. "She doesn't approve of me?"

"No, of me. Lately, I've been anti-commitment—"

"I think we're on the same page," Sunny said with a seductive timbre.

Normally, Noel would've been thrilled to hear those words, but before Sunny interrupted her, she was about to say that she was no longer interested in temporary hookups.

"So technically, we wouldn't be dating?" Sunny added.

"That's a very tempting offer."

"Good, I'll call you."

"Hey! We got an idea," Harper said as she and Lydia ran onto the patio. "Let's all go to the haunted cornfield ride next weekend."

Noel was captivated by what she saw in Sunny's eyes. "The...what?" she asked, unable to look away.

"In White Castle, they have a place that does hayrides in a haunted cornfield." Harper put her finger beneath Noel's chin and forced her to make eye contact. "It was Lydia's idea. We think it'll be fun."

"And your inclusion of the ancients is because you want us to finance this excursion?" Noel said with a sneer.

"Well that, and I'm not allowed to drive outside of Baton Rouge, unless that rule has changed?" Lydia gazed at Sunny with a hopeful expression.

Sunny shook her head. "That rule still stands."

"We could do one of those wandering adventures you talked about earlier, make a whole day of it," Lydia persisted. "You just said you missed that."

"Um…are you interested?" Sunny turned to Noel.

"I'm game."

Noel and Harper stood side by side in the driveway waving as Sunny and Lydia drove away. The minute they were out of sight, aunt and niece turned on each other.

"You little shit! You knew exactly what you were doing when you brought up Glynn!"

Harper shimmied her shoulders as she quoted Noel sounding like she was about to gag. "'You're so pretty.' You can't help yourself! You're like a robot designed to hit on everything."

"It was a genuine compliment. She's a very pretty woman!"

"You can't take your eyes off her." Harper waved her arms around. "You touched her every chance you got." She poked Noel in the chest. "You're making a move, and I asked you not to."

Noel scrubbed a hand through her hair. "Most people your age don't care if their parents get along or not. So what if I dated Sunny? So what if it doesn't work out?"

Harper clamped her lips together tightly before she said, "I told Lydia you were a player, and she still seems to be trying to play matchmaker. She was all excited about the four of us going on that hayride."

"You told her what?" Noel asked as her blood boiled.

"You don't get it. This is important to Lydia, she wants her mother to find someone to be happy with." Harper lowered her voice. "You know that's not you."

"That hurt."

"I'm not trying to be mean. This is important to Lydia, so it's important to me."

"We need to talk."

"I need to cool down." Harper backed up a step. "I didn't mean to hurt your feelings. I'll see you tomorrow."

Noel watched Harper jog across the backyard and up the stairs of the garage apartment, still stinging from the rebuke.

By Wednesday, Sunny began to fear that Noel was put off by her offer. The notion embarrassed her, and she wasn't sure what disappointed her more—the missed opportunity or the pain of rejection. She'd begun sending a string of texts on Monday afternoon that had thus far gone unanswered.

She blinked when a file folder landed on her desk in front of her with a smack. "Were you sleeping? I called your name three times."

"My mind was somewhere else." Sunny tried to keep annoyance out of her tone and opened the folder. Chris Chappel, one of her inspectors, took a seat prepared to answer questions. "You were out early this morning."

"Four a.m. I don't know why incidents that happen in the wee hours are always when I'm on call. I'm beginning to suspect a conspiracy."

"This seems cut-and-dried, the harm done to the dock was the fault of the tankerman who failed to adjust moorings to the barge he was loading and the dockman who wasn't paying attention. Negligence on both sides here." Sunny scanned the report further. "No damage to the barge, no product spill. Good for me, less paperwork." She closed the folder. "We're done here. Go home and get some sleep," she said when her phone vibrated on her desk, and she caught a glimpse of Noel's name.

"Did you get a chance to review the injury report on the dock three injury again?"

Few things grated Sunny's nerves more than to be in the middle of a discussion and have someone looking at their phone or texting. Since they weren't allowed to be used outside of the safety building, everyone seemed to want to catch up on their messages when they meeting with her. So she enacted a strict no phone use policy in her office. She couldn't very well break her own rule, but it was killing her not to read Noel's message.

"I—" Sunny's curiosity grew when another text hit her phone. "It's on my agenda."

Chris sank deeper into his chair. "That whole thing pisses me off. I don't know how the dockman thinks he can dispute my findings. If he'd been wearing steel toes, that pipe would've bounced off his boot. And in the dock shack, there was a pair of sneakers with a big slice in the toe. I took a picture of them, it's in the report. He wasn't wearing the appropriate gear, period."

"Snapping the photo was a good idea. I'll have a look at it. Go get some rest."

Another text vibrated the phone when Chris said, "Another thing, when Brewer's on shift, the camera mysteriously malfunctions. Not every shift, but every so often. Curly told me that Brewer has issues with a bunion. I think when it flares up, he kills the camera and puts on shoes that aren't regulation. I wanna put another camera on that dock that he doesn't know—"

"That's a moot point right now because he's out for two weeks. We'll discuss it when he comes back on shift. Now go home."

"Hey, did you see—"

"Dude, go home!" Sunny cleared her throat and smiled. "I'm worried about you. You've got big bags under your eyes. How bad would it be if someone in safety had an accident because they were fatigued?"

"Good point," Chris said as he stood. "I'll be back in the morning unless I get something tonight, then you'll find me on the couch in the reception area when you get in."

Sunny pointed at the door, and Chris finally complied. The second he stepped into the hallway, she grabbed her phone and began to read.

"Sorry I haven't answered sooner. I'm free after ten tonight.

I realize that's kinda late on a work night, but I have nosy neighbors that should be asleep then.

I'm between patients, so if you text and don't get a response, it's because I'm drilling a tooth or removing a fishbone.

Sunny breathed out a sigh of relief and typed her reply. *I'll see you at ten thirty.*

She set the phone on her desk and stared at her computer screen. A moment of clarity tried to rush in. After Tamara died, Sunny had not felt even a twinge of connection with the women she dated, but when she sat there painting that stupid pumpkin, she felt a slight tingle. She'd come to believe that she would never feel the magic that she had with Tamara ever again. Part of her didn't want to.

Noel had no sooner pulled into her driveway that evening when her mother called. "Come eat, I got leftover roast out the wazoo."

"Are you spying on me?"

"I'm in the bush burning one, I saw you pass. Hey, the Schulameyers bought a new TV, and it's huge. Their house is the size of a cracker box, their car is a piece of crap, but they buy a TV the size of a Buick. Go figure."

"Put the cigarette out, I'll be over after I change," Noel said as she climbed out of her car.

"I'll have you a plate made by the time you get here."

"Not too much, Momma. I try not to eat heavy at night, and lately, I've been breaking that habit."

"You could use a few pounds. You got no ass."

"My pants say differently. See you in a few."

Noel went inside and debated a shower but decided to wait until after dinner. She changed into a pair of shorts and a sweatshirt, then put fresh linens on her bed. As she turned the covers back, she struggled with her decision to text Sunny earlier that day. She didn't want Sunny to think she was uninterested because she was very interested. Noel also wondered—hoped—that Sunny might turn into one of those women who enthusiastically agreed to no strings but changed their minds later. What she did know about Sunny Chase, she liked. Then there was Harper. Noel didn't want to risk damaging their relationship, especially now. Something was up with Harper, and Noel believed it was Lydia. Perhaps Harper hadn't realized it yet, but she appeared to be smitten.

Noel made the short hike to her parents' house. Her dad was already seated at the kitchen table as she stepped inside the back door. "There's my baby girl," he said and held out his arms.

Noel gave him a hug and a kiss. "You didn't take the boat out today?"

He waved a hand dismissively. "I decided that I'd rather be home with my kitten."

"Bullshit," Inez said as she set a plate in front of him. "I told your father either he fixes the porch or he could sleep in Jeff's boat. Noel, sit."

"I can fix my own drink and plate, Momma."

"You better sit down, she's in a mood," Joe whispered.

"I already made your plate like I said I would. What do you want to drink?"

"Water is fine." Noel took a seat next to her father.

When Inez returned to the table, it was with a glass of wine and a plate piled so high it nearly met Noel's chin. "What you don't eat, you take."

"Thanks, Mom."

Inez set her plate on the other side of Joe and took a seat. It held a dainty piece of roast and one potato. "I called Mary, but she said she was taking Harper for pizza. I got half a cow goin' here, and they go out." Inez threw up a hand. "Why do you look so tense?"

"Long day." Noel tried to smile as her mind swirled.

"I gotta tell ya, I like Lydia and Sunny. Lydia's kinda quiet, but I think she'll come outta her shell once she gets to know us. Your mom told me that Sunny's a lesbian, and she's a looker. You gonna ask her out?"

"No, I don't think so, Dad."

"Why not?" Inez asked with disappointment. "She's got a good job, seems to have her shit together, she's loyal like a dog, but I think what you got on your hands, Noel, is a cat."

"Oh, hey, Will Lisbon and his wife are having a boy," Noel said suddenly, hoping her subject change would catch.

Joe raised his wineglass. "Willie finally put the stem on the little apple. After how many girls?"

"Four," Noel answered with a smile. "He says they're done now, but Chloe is taking the wait and see attitude."

Inez was like a bloodhound on a scent. "What's wrong with this one? Her feet didn't look big, she smelled good."

"You know what? I'm not comfortable dating the mother of one of Harper's friends." Noel shrugged. "That's it, end of discussion."

"I thought you two looked good together, and you seemed to get along so well. Baby, take a chance."

"Mom, let it go, please."

"On another note, I fixed that damn spindle, and I think I'm gonna paint the porch black tomorrow with gold trim," Joe said, coming to Noel's aid. "I saw one of those big metal Saints medallions in the store, it'd look good on a black wall."

Inez snarled. "You who is wearing red shorts with a green shirt is gonna decorate the porch?"

"What? I'm ready for Christmas. Am I not still cute to you?"

Inez melted a little bit. "You'll always be adorable to me, but you're not painting the porch black."

Noel leaned against the wall with her arms folded as she watched Sunny pull into her driveway. She'd left the lights on in the kitchen, but the rest of the house was dark. This didn't feel like the casual arrangements she was used to, and Noel realized that she'd already developed a real attachment to Sunny. She knew if Sunny came in and they talked, she might admit the truth. She knew that was the last thing someone who was looking for no strings wanted to hear, so she prepared to take what was being offered.

Sunny barely had time to knock when Noel opened the door and took her by the hand. The kiss Noel delivered was hot. Sunny seemed stunned for only a second before she gave into it completely. Noel pushed her against the wall, closed the door with her foot, flipped the lock, and slipped her hand beneath

Sunny's shirt. Her pulse pounded as she felt warm soft skin under her fingertips. The muscles of Sunny's abdomen fluttered at her touch, and she released a soft moan as she fisted her hands in Noel's shirt.

Sunny hadn't expected to be taken just inside the door, but it was a welcome surprise. She wasn't wasting any time, either, and tugged on the shirt in her hands until Noel broke the kiss long enough to allow it to be pulled over her head. Sunny was delighted that Noel had not bothered with a bra. She struggled to get her hands between their bodies, wanting to feel the supple flesh. Sunny's eyes flew open when Noel trailed kisses down her cheek and softly bit when her lips found her neck.

"You smell so good," Noel breathed against her neck.

Sunny didn't want to talk, didn't want to be distracted from what she had committed herself to doing. She pulled Noel's mouth to hers and kissed her roughly while Noel unfastened her jeans. In hindsight, Sunny wished she'd worn something easier to remove. The snug denim barely moved as Noel tried to push it down her hips.

Noel's mouth was left wanting when Sunny suddenly slid down and took her nipple into her mouth. She planted both hands on the wall, legs trembling with arousal as Sunny sucked and nibbled. There were rules that Noel had about these encounters, but they refused to pass her lips as Sunny sank lower and jerked her shorts to the floor. She stepped backward, bringing Sunny along with her toward the bedroom, their mouths joined as they crept slowly.

Sunny's shirt was unbuttoned and fell to the floor by the time they reached the doorway. The sound of their labored breathing and out-of-control kisses seemed to echo off the walls. Noel removed Sunny's bra and tossed it. Their bare skin brushed for only a second before Noel gently pushed Sunny down and yanked her jeans, underwear, and shoes off seemingly in one motion. Sunny had one sock on and one dangling off her toe when Noel climbed on top of her. Her senses were on overload beneath Noel's weight. Noel's skin felt smooth and hot beneath her hand. Her mouth was inciting a riot inside of Sunny as it trailed kisses along her jaw. She could feel how wet Noel was as their bodies pressed together. Noel's moan sent jolts of electricity through her as she raised her knees higher, opening herself up to the steady rhythm of Noel grinding into her.

It was normally all about the orgasm for Noel. She enjoyed the rush of being the cause of that moment of extreme pleasure, and she was always in a hurry to make that happen. But she found herself wanting to explore Sunny. She wanted to know all of her secrets, and she was about to break her cardinal rule about hookups as she began to kiss her way down Sunny's chest.

Sunny sucked in a breath between her teeth when Noel's mouth closed on one of her nipples. The pleasure and the pain of it were exquisite. The fingers of one hand dug into Noel's shoulder, her other hand was in her hair. She dug her heels into the bed as Noel drifted lower.

"So soft, so beautiful," Noel whispered against the skin of Sunny's abdomen as she tasted and craved what lie ahead. She moved closer to what she considered forbidden fruit, longing for just a taste, knowing that she would have her fill. Sunny hadn't uttered a word or released a moan since they reached the bedroom, but when Noel's mouth opened over her, it forced a helpless cry from her throat. Noel sighed as her tongue slipped into her.

It had been so long since Sunny felt such intense pleasure. She felt overcome by it, unable to do or say anything as Noel stroked her into madness. Her hips moved on their own, shying away from pressure she wasn't ready to take. Noel allowed her to dictate what she wanted for a while, then tightened her grip on Sunny's thighs as she took control, demanding what she wanted. Sunny's heels dug into the bed as Noel pushed her closer.

Noel clamped her eyes shut as Sunny stilled, knowing what was about to happen next. She kept Sunny suspended in that moment for as long as she could and listened as Sunny released an explosive breath as her legs grew weak. "Oh...Noel." Sunny panted out as the tremors continued to burst against the flat of Noel's tongue.

Sunny was filled with a hunger. She wanted more orgasms, and she wanted Noel's. She tugged on Noel's hair gently until she began to move back up her body. As Noel slid up, Sunny slipped down until she could take a nipple into her mouth. She lavished it only for a moment before she urged Noel higher. Noel was nearly on her hands and knees as Sunny slipped lower.

"I'll turn around if you—" Noel gasped when Sunny's tongue slipped into her wetness. Sunny grasped her hips, letting Noel know that she didn't intend for her to move. She watched in the dim light as Noel arched her back and craned her head back, wishing she could see her face. Noel moaned as she covered Sunny's hands with her own.

It had been so long since Noel let anyone do this to her. Foolishly, she tried to think back to the last time Brenna loved her like this and couldn't remember. Sunny wasn't shy about taking what she wanted. She worked Noel with her tongue until she trembled. Noel bent forward and gripped the sheets in her fists, her hips moving of their own volition. Sunny's hold became firmer as she took from Noel.

Noel's eyes slowly closed as flames of white-hot pleasure fanned out over her lower body. Her breath caught in her throat. She'd become still, unable to move. She gasped as though she were drowning and pulled away from Sunny's intense touch.

Noel fell against the headboard as she caught her breath and gazed at Sunny, who lay flat on her back, her arms spread wide. Her chest moved up and down rapidly. "Come here," Noel whispered. Sunny sat up and scooted as though she were going to sit next to Noel. "No, straddle my legs." Sunny did as Noel asked. "Relax." Noel slipped her hand between Sunny's legs. "Put your weight on me."

They were face to face, and Sunny's eyes had adjusted to the darkness. She stared into Noel's, unable to see clearly. She didn't trust herself to hold on to Noel's shoulders. She knew what was about to happen; the anticipation made her grip the headboard instead.

"Kiss me."

Sunny's lips had barely touched Noel's when Noel entered her. They both gasped. One arm circled Sunny's waist as Noel pushed deeper into her. "How far will you let me take you?" Noel asked against her mouth.

Sunny was unsure what Noel was asking until she slipped another finger inside of her. She rested her head against Noel's as she caught her breath after another jolt of arousal coursed through her body. Sunny's lips moved, but nothing came out.

"I won't do anything you're uncomfortable with," Noel said breathlessly and slipped another finger inside.

Sunny shuddered with all she wanted to say. Her voice was hoarse when she uttered, "Take me as far as you want." She clamped her eyes shut when Noel gently pulled out of her and pushed her down on her back.

Noel's hands trembled as she pulled Sunny's knees up and spread her legs wide. She knelt between them, leaned down, and kissed Sunny before whispering in her ear. "If it gets to be too much, tell me to stop."

It won't, Sunny thought as she gripped the back of Noel's neck. Noel slipped two fingers inside of her and worked her slowly until Sunny's hips demanded more. Sunny listened to Noel's erratic breathing against her ear, wondering if Noel would submit to the same, and hoped she would.

Noel slipped her tongue deep into Sunny's mouth at the same time she added two more fingers. Sunny was so wet, she took her with ease. She took her slowly and deeper. "Talk to me," she said against Sunny's mouth when she broke the kiss.

"I want this," Sunny breathed out. Noel's lips trembled against hers, and Sunny wondered who was going to come first. Her hand went to Noel's breast and captured a nipple between her fingers. Noel moaned into her mouth as she kissed her again.

Sunny craned her head back and sucked in a breath between her teeth as Noel entered her fully. "Oh, Noel," she groaned. "Go slow."

"I will," Noel whispered as she showered Sunny's neck and chest with kisses.

"Promise…promise…you'll let me do this," Sunny said as she began to lose control.

"Not tonight," Noel said against the skin of Sunny's stomach. "But the next time, yes."

Sunny shuddered as Noel's mouth trailed lower over her skin. Noel's thrusts were slow and gentle. "Don't think that I'll forget." Sunny moaned as Noel's tongue flicked over her. She felt hypersensitive. "I'll come quickly."

"I won't let you."

"I want to."

"I know." Noel's response was almost a whimper. Sunny was almost completely undone. Her restraint was fading, and Noel wanted to experience the minute she completely lost it.

"Noel," she whispered over and over as she filled her hands with the sheets. Noel was grinding against the bed, unable to stop herself. "I want to be the one to make you come."

"You are," she said as she closed her mouth over Sunny. Noel whimpered as Sunny's back cleared the bed. Her cry shattered the stillness and Noel along with it.

"I'd venture to say we have great sexual chemistry."

Noel looked at the clock on the stand beside her bed. "It's two o'clock, we've been perfecting it for almost four hours. Between the two of us, we've drunk a gallon of water, and I still feel dehydrated."

Sunny lay with her head on Noel's shoulder. She was snuggly and warm and wanted to stay there. "We're going to be miserable in the morning…well, later in the morning. I hate to, but I have to go."

Noel kissed the top of Sunny's head. "I know."

"I can't do this again tonight. I have to catch up on sleep, I'm not young like you are."

"How old am I?"

Sunny kissed Noel's collarbone and rose up on her elbow. "You're thirty-five, Harper told me."

"How old are you?" Noel tucked a lock of hair behind Sunny's ear.

"Six years older than you."

Noel released a mock gasp. "I've been cradle-robbed. You sure don't look forty-one, and you don't make love like it, either."

Sunny slowly got up and began looking for her clothes. "How many forty-somethings have you had?"

"A couple, but what I really mean is, you have the stamina of a twenty-year-old."

Sunny grinned as she untangled her pants and sneakers. "I take that as a huge compliment, thank you." She stared at the floor for a moment. "This is an interesting rug."

"Yeah, it's a basketball court. I've got a goal on the back of my door."

Sunny looked around, taking note of things she hadn't really noticed before. The thirty-five-year-old "coochie catcher" had the bedroom of a teenaged boy. Her four-poster wrought iron bed was the only adult thing in there. A fake stuffed moose mounted on the wall stared back at her with plastic eyes. Noel's three-drawer dresser was a rowboat stood up on its stern. Sunny was about to ask if her decorator was still in elementary school, but she decided against it.

"So I guess I'll see you again on Saturday?" Noel got up and slipped on her robe. Is ten that morning okay?"

"That sounds great." Sunny pulled her pants up and stepped into her sneakers. "If the weather's good, we can take the Jeep and go topless."

Noel's gaze swept over Sunny naked from the waist up. "I like that idea."

Sunny finished dressing, and Noel walked her to the door. Noel wrapped her arms around her waist and kissed her. Even after hours of sex, it still stirred desire within Sunny. She pulled away reluctantly. "I'll see you Saturday."

"Text me when you get home, so I'll know you made it safely."

"I will." Sunny planted a quick kiss on Noel's lips. "Good morning."

Noel watched as Sunny got into her car and drove away. She went into the kitchen and switched off the lights after drinking two more glasses of water. She went back to her bedroom and remade the destroyed bed feeling like the needy one who wanted to wrap Sunny with as many strings as she could.

Chapter 11

"Are you gay?"

Harper was completely taken aback by the question and pissed that Corey asked in her in the school hallway where they were surrounded by everyone. "You act like you don't know me here, and now you want to discuss my personal life? Piss off, Corey."

"Everyone's talking about it, and it's cool if you are. I just wanna know."

Harper opened her locker in Corey's face. "I'm sure you know I could give a shit about what people think."

"Lydia's cute," Corey said as she peeked around the door.

"Are you just looking for a confirmation, so you can go back and tell everyone that I'm a lesbian?"

"Yeah, basically. People ask me questions, and I don't wanna spread rumors."

Harper closed the door to her locker and met Corey's gaze. "Go back and tell them it's none of their damn business." She turned and left Corey in her wake. Her friends Ashlynn and Selene had already asked the same question, right after they bitched about being ignored. Both of them promised to be very accepting if Harper would've wanted to include Lydia in their circle, but she didn't. She was selfish with her time when it came to Lydia.

As friends went, Ashlynn and Selene were on a completely different plane compared to Lydia. Conversations with her buddies were about boys, school events, gossip, and general bullshit. With Lydia, Harper talked about her dreams.

Sometimes, they didn't talk at all, and there were no complaints or questions as to why she was quiet. Lydia was a soul friend, someone who understood Harper, and she loved that. For the first time in her young life, she felt connected to someone on a level she didn't think existed among her peers. Lydia didn't care about being popular or concern herself with social circles. She had her own mind, did her own thing, and Harper could totally identify with that.

Harper pushed through the double doors at the end of the hall, and a cool breeze swept over her skin as sunlight temporarily blinded her. Lydia parked in the same place every day at the far end of the student lot. Harper hurried, though she knew Lydia wouldn't leave without her. But as she drew closer, she saw Lydia sitting on the tailgate of her truck, and she wasn't alone.

Aubrey Malone stood close by occasionally flipping her blond hair. She reached out and touched one of the bracelets on Lydia's wrist. Like most girls at school, Aubrey claimed to be bi because it drove the guys insane. But Aubrey had taken it one step further and had kissed Violet Crochet in front of an audience to prove her point. This wasn't the first time Harper had noticed Aubrey paying attention to Lydia. She made a special effort to say hi when they passed in the halls, always with the damn hair flip that had begun to annoy Harper. Aubrey also had a boyfriend and had dated a lot of guys at school, including Mason, who bragged that he was going broke buying rubbers to keep up with Aubrey's demands. It incensed Harper that Aubrey had obviously set her sights on Lydia.

Lydia noticed Harper coming toward them and smiled, a genuine "I'm happy to see you smile." Harper took that to mean Lydia needed rescuing. She was more than happy to oblige. "Aubrey, don't you have something to blow?" Harper said as she walked up, opened the passenger's door to Lydia's truck, and tossed her book sack inside, a symbol of laying claim in her mind.

"Whoa," Aubrey said with an expression of shock and anger. "Retract the claws, babe. We were just talking."

Harper folded her arms. "And now you're done. Lydia, you ready?"

Lydia looked stunned as she hopped off the tailgate and slammed it shut. "Yeah."

"I'll see you around, Lydia," Aubrey said, keeping an eye on Harper for a moment before she walked off.

Lydia laughed when she and Harper climbed into the truck. "I take it you don't like her."

"She's a panty dropper that will use you to get the attention of the guys." Harper slammed her door. "As if she doesn't have enough already. Are you into her?"

"She's cute, but no," Lydia said as she backed out of her parking spot. "I know what she is."

Lydia's admission burned in the pit of Harper's stomach. "How could you think she's cute?"

Lydia shrugged. "I just do."

"I thought you were the type to judge a person based on what's on the inside instead of being like everyone else and going all googly-eyed over someone with big tits and legs that're always open."

Lydia's brows rose above her sunglasses. "Wow. That's harsh. Do you hate her because of something she did to you or because she gets around?"

"Here's the deal. I think it sucks that even in this age that some girls are still looked down on because they have the same sexual appetites as guys. That's not my problem with her. I hate that she uses people to get what she wants. She says she's bi, but she's really not. Whether you sleep with her or not, she'll tell everyone y'all did because it makes the guys want her more, and she enjoys throwing that up in other girls' faces."

"Did she take your boyfriend?" Lydia asked gently.

"No! I know you get this, Lydia, you're smart. She's a user, and I don't like that she obviously wants to get her nasty hands on you."

"I got it."

"Why are you smiling—you're laughing?"

Lydia snorted. "'Don't you have something to blow?' That's classic," she said as her body shook with laughter.

Harper frowned. "I get my sharp tongue from Nana."

Lydia sobered and cleared her throat. "Just for the record, I'd never do Aubrey. She's not my type."

Harper found herself satisfied with that statement, and her anger began to ebb. "What is your type?"

"Not her."

"Could you be more specific?"

Lydia thought for a minute. "I'm really not attracted to redheads, but I'm not saying I wouldn't date one on that alone. Real...she just has to be real."

"As in not a blowup doll?"

"Oh, you're a tool today," Lydia said with a laugh. "Where do you want to go?"

"The park."

Lydia flipped on her turn signal and made a left. "What's your type?"

"I really don't know if I have one. I'm the least sexual person I know. I don't really get excited about anyone. Corey thinks that soccer player David Beckham is the hottest guy on the planet. She told me once that she gets herself off while staring at the poster of him on her wall. I don't get it."

"Have you ever been in love?"

Harper sighed. "Not even close. Have you?"

"I thought I was once," Lydia said as she turned into the lot of the park. After she killed the engine, she reached into her backpack and pulled out a can of juice and a snack bar.

Harper watched her and asked, "Why don't you eat lunch?"

"I don't like what they serve."

Harper pushed open her door. "I wish I was a picky eater, maybe I'd be skinny."

"You're perfect," Lydia said as she met Harper in front of the truck, then pointed to a grassy spot in the sun. "Let's go over there."

"Finish telling me about thinking you were in love."

"It's stupid." Lydia broke the bar in half and handed a piece to Harper.

"I'm not taking part of the only food you've had all day."

"It's not. Ethan cooks for me every morning. Today I had a bacon and egg sandwich with strawberries. I don't really get hungry in the middle of the day. At night, I eat like a pig. Take it."

"Thanks," Harper said as she accepted the piece. "So tell me."

"It was a crush, but I thought I was in love. She probably didn't even know my name, but I was crazy about Ashleigh. She played the drums in the marching band at my old school. She was in my English class, and she used to write the most frickin' awesome papers. One time, we had to write one on who we thought we were, and I remember a line she wrote, 'I wake up wanting to be someone else every day, and every night, I'm disappointed that I'm still just me.' I totally identified then because I was realizing that I was gay, and I didn't want to be. I just wanted to wake up and be like everybody else. But at the same time, I couldn't stop wanting her."

Harper sat in the grass and folded her legs. "When did you finally accept it?"

Lydia shrugged. "I dunno. I just woke up someone else one morning. I guess I got tired of worrying about not being accepted. Mom talked to me about it a lot, which made it easier." She opened her juice and passed the can to Harper. "I was pissed at her for a while, though, because I wanted to blame her for making me this way. She always told me that just because she was gay didn't mean I would be and that she'd always be happy with me for who I was. But I thought I'd caught it from her and Ethan like a disease."

"Maybe it's genetic. Noel kinda blows that theory because everybody in our family is straight or at least the ones we knew of before us. Nana says people didn't come out in her day or before, so we could've had a rainbow baby in a closet somewhere."

"I think it's cool that your whole family accepts her and you do that thing y'all do before you eat."

"I do, too," Harper said with a smile. "Oh! I got you something." She leaned back and pulled a leather strap from the pocket of her uniform pants. I got this a few years ago when we went to Florida. I used to wear it a lot, but I think it'll match your bracelets, and it'll look better on you."

Lydia took the necklace and admired the pewter dolphin pendant. "I love it, thanks."

"If you slide the two knots in the cord, it makes it bigger and you can slip it over your head, then tighten it to the length you want."

Lydia did as Harper instructed and slipped it on. "You have to take one of my bracelets now. Which one would you like?"

Harper smiled as she gazed at the pendant lying against Lydia's skin. "It's a gift, I don't expect anything in return."

"The bracelet is my gift to you, so pick one." Lydia held up her wrists and blinked rapidly. "Unless you don't like them."

"No, I do. You pick it, though."

Harper had always admired the leather band with rainbow beads woven into it and was surprised when Lydia began to work it free of her wrist because she'd never told Lydia so. What stunned her more was her excitement over wearing it, not just because she liked it but because it was Lydia's.

Britney Spears was rocking a broom mic as she belted out *Oops...I Did It Again* in the iconic red leather jumpsuit. Ethan had the makeup and all the steps. Tobi lay on the couch bathing, only giving him an occasional glance as the music blared and he danced. Drunk with exhaustion, all Sunny could do was stand there and watch the spectacle, her laughter drowned out by the music.

Ethan whirled and began the chorus. "Oops I—shit!" he screamed and grabbed his chest. He snatched the remote off the coffee table and silenced the music. "You're home early," he said calmly.

"Sorry to disturb you." Sunny grinned as her gaze swept over a paunchy sixty-year-old male body wedged into a skin-tight suit. "Did you use a shoe horn or Vaseline to get into that thing?"

Ethan jutted his chin. "Baby oil, helps the leather slide and protects me from chaffing. Why do you look like someone punched you in both eyes?"

"Have you heard from Lydia?"

Ethan nodded. "She texted me after school and said she was going to hang out with Harper for a while. She'll be home at dinner time. Answer the question."

"I'm exhausted. I didn't get any sleep last night."

"Insomnia?" Ethan asked with a sympathetic tone as he followed Sunny to her bedroom. "I have some sleeping pills prescribed to me, but I can't take them. One time, I dreamed that I had long hair, and I brushed it all night. The next morning when I woke up, I was sitting in my chair at the vanity with a wig on my head, and it was half bald. They may not have that effect on you, and your hair is kinda thick anyway."

Sunny sat on the bench in front of her bed and began unlacing her work boots, which she normally took off at the door. Her forgetfulness was a testament to how tired she actually was. "I don't have insomnia." She gazed up at Ethan with a huge grin, her voice growing louder as she said, "I had sex for hours last night. It was awesome!"

"For—hours?" Ethan threw a hand on his hip. "We men are cursed."

"I sneaked out after y'all went to bed."

"And you're happy?"

Sunny stared at him incredulously. "I lost track of the orgasms. I'm numb from the waist down. Yes, I'm happy."

"For hours." Ethan shook his head slowly as if trying to comprehend it.

Sunny held up a hand. "Don't rain on my afterglow by trying to get into my head. I'm going to take a nap right after I shower. Would you wake me up if I'm still asleep by dinner?"

"You won't sleep tonight."

"Oh, yes, I will." Sunny stood slowly. "I hope I can undress myself."

"Don't ask me to help. I don't want to see anything that's had that much action," Ethan quipped as he walked to the door.

"You're nasty."

"So are you, sugar."

Sunny stripped out of her clothes, took a quick shower, and managed to shrug on a T-shirt before she fell into bed. She'd talked a good game to Ethan, but there was a part of her that felt as though she had acted too hastily. Noel was a passionate lover, but at times during their escapade, she was extremely affectionate. Sweet touches and soft kisses stimulated something that wasn't on the outside of her body. As she drove home that morning, Sunny wondered if maybe she'd ironically told the right woman that she didn't want commitments.

Noel ate cereal for dinner, showered, and planned to be in bed by eight, but she ran into a snag when Harper showed up on her doorstep. "You got a minute?" Harper asked.

The look on Harper's face made it impossible for Noel to say no. "For you, always," she said with a smile, but on the inside, she worried that Harper had spotted Sunny's car in her driveway the night before. "Okay, just throw it out there."

Harper took a seat on the edge of a chair, set her elbows on her knees, and clasped her hands in front of her. She didn't say anything for a moment or two. Noel stared at the bracelet on her arm. She'd seen Lydia wearing it and wondered why Harper was in possession of it now.

"When did you first know you were gay?" Harper asked as she stared at the floor.

Noel blinked rapidly at the unexpected question. "It seems to me that I always knew. I had crushes on my teachers and other girls in elementary school. It wasn't until junior high that I realized it actually meant something. I do have friends that were adults before they discovered their sexual orientation. Are you questioning yours?"

"Yeah." Harper toyed with the bracelet. "I'm questioning everything right now. I don't know where I'm at. Today at school, I saw Lydia talking to a skank, and I was, like, immediately pissed off. Lydia's not interested in her, but I started thinking, what if she does meet a girl she likes? I don't wanna lose her, and I can't decide if it bothers me because she's a great friend and I won't get to spend as much time with her or if it's something more."

"Have you ever been attracted to girls?"

Harper shrugged. "Not to anyone. I don't drool over guys, but I don't do that when it comes to girls, either."

Noel mulled that for a moment, then asked, "Are you physically attracted to Lydia?"

"I don't know, that's the problem. I like her style, that whole wild hair bohemian thing she's got going on. I think it's cool that she does her own thing, she doesn't act or dress just to fit in." Harper continued to avoid eye contact. "When I'm with her, I feel…a part of something special."

"Does this scare you?"

Harper finally met Noel's gaze and shook her head. "It just confuses me. My jealousy today when I saw Lydia with that girl made me start to question why I haven't really been attracted to anyone. I was kinda hoping you could use your gaydar superpowers and tell me if I'm gay."

Noel smiled. "I can't diagnose you, baby. You'll have to draw your own conclusions, but you won't be alone. You have our entire family behind you, regardless. My advice is to try not to let this stress you. Be honest with yourself, take your time, and examine your feelings. There's no rush."

"Okay, yes, I am scared," Harper said emphatically. "Not of discovering that I'm gay, but finding out I do have a thing for Lydia, and she doesn't like me that way."

Noel pursed her lips. "That's a very common fear that most everyone faces."

Harper stood. "Don't tell anyone we had this conversation, please. I'm not ready to face questions from Mom and Nana yet."

Noel got up, too, and pulled Harper into her arms. "It stays between us. You know you always have my shoulder and my ear."

"I do." Harper squeezed Noel and let her go. "Thanks, I gotta get back. I told Mom I wanted to borrow your purple high tops."

"My Converse, are you crazy?"

Harper threw a hand on her hip. "They're sneakers, you're not gonna die. I'll give them back to you tomorrow, unharmed."

When Harper left, Noel stood at her kitchen window and watched over the neighboring fences until she saw Harper on the stairs of the garage apartment. Noel sighed as the floodlights outside switched off, indicating that Harper was inside. She empathized with Harper because she was dealing with her own conflicting emotions.

The encounter with Sunny stayed on her mind, and she went into her bedroom and climbed into sheets that still held Sunny's perfume and contemplated what she was doing. Noel wondered if perhaps she was a little arrogant. Normally after a night with a woman, she would receive texts or calls from those seeking the promise of another night. Sunny hadn't done either of those things. The other surprising and equally disconcerting issue was, Noel couldn't wait for Saturday to come, so she could spend the day with Sunny.

"I'm losing my cat fur," she said miserably. "I'm becoming a puppy."

Chapter 12

"I think you should pack a picnic basket," Ethan said as he watched Lydia and Sunny lower the top on the Jeep.

Sunny shook her head. "That basket would have to be huge to feed four people, and you know there isn't a lot of cargo room."

"Eating out is part of the fun," Lydia added and kissed Ethan on the cheek.

Ethan planted both hands on his hips. "Both of you are positively giddy."

"It's a gorgeous day, and we're looking forward to being out in it," Sunny said with a smile. "I wish you would come with us."

"No roof, no thank you." Ethan shielded his eyes from the sun and watched as Noel and Harper came up the driveway, both of them grinning like fools, too.

Noel parked behind Lydia's truck, got out of her car, and put a red ball cap on her head backward. "I am ready to ride, to where I know not, and therein lies the excitement."

Ethan pointed at Sunny. "She's every bit the dork you are."

"That's right." Sunny grinned and held up her fist. Noel bumped it.

"Now listen to me, ladies." Ethan clutched his bad hand and held it to his chest. "Wear your seat belts. Be aware of your surroundings at all times. Don't talk to strangers. Keep your mouths closed or you may eat a bug."

"Yes, Grandma," Lydia said with a laugh as she and Harper climbed into the backseat. "I call DJ, I brought my iPod."

Ethan gave Noel the eye. "You take care of my girls. My whole life is in that Jeep."

"I promise...Grandma."

"I'm the oldest on this trip. I'm in charge," Sunny said with a smile and kissed him on the cheek. "We'll be back late, but you can always call if you feel the need to check on us." She handed Noel the keys. "You're in the driver's seat."

"See, I'm really in charge," Noel whispered and winked at Ethan as she climbed in. "Okay, what do we want to see?"

"Something creepy," Harper shouted.

Lydia threw her arms up. "I'm down with the scary."

Sunny shrugged. "I'm game for anything."

Noel tried not to read too much into that statement and backed slowly out of the driveway while everyone waved at Ethan. "I know where there's an old graveyard on the west bank, which is on the way to White Castle."

"That works," Harper said.

Once they got onto the interstate, it was impossible to have a conversation over the wind noise without yelling. Lydia had chosen what she considered "road songs," all of which included thundering bass. Noel glanced into the rearview and grinned at the two girls dancing in the backseat, their hands in the air. Sunny nodded to the beat with her hair in a ponytail, the sun on her face.

Noel had a compulsion to touch her. She wanted to feel the warmth of Sunny's skin and wondered if the real draw was that she simply wanted something she couldn't have. It was a sobering thought that she mulled as she drove.

They crossed over the Mississippi River Bridge, and Noel took a winding and narrow road through cornfields. The music fell silent suddenly when Sunny turned off her stereo to grumbles in the backseat. "How is it that you know of a spooky graveyard in the middle of nowhere?"

"My brother found it when he was looking for private places to take his girlfriends," Noel answered with a smirk. "He claims while out here one night, he and his date saw a woman in a white dress wandering among the tombstones."

"Always a white dress or flowing gown. Why does no one ever say they saw a ghost sporting a pair of jeans and a T-shirt?" Sunny asked.

Noel shrugged. "I'd still be freaked out if I saw one in a pink tutu."

Harper leaned her head between the seats. "You know what else is scary? I'm getting hungry."

Sunny pushed her back playfully, and Noel looked at Harper in the rearview. "You ate breakfast an hour ago."

"Hey, I'm just giving you a heads-up that after we check out the graveyard, I'm gonna need food." Harper smiled sweetly and fluttered her eyelids.

Noel slowed when they came to a cropping of trees and turned onto an overgrown gravel road. Sunny gazed up at the moss hanging from the branches above. "Okay, this is creepy even in the daylight. If a date brought me out here in the dark, it would be the last."

"In more ways than one." Lydia released an evil-sounding cackle.

Sunny turned to Noel with a wry smile. "She gets her flair for drama from Ethan."

"This from a woman who put on a curly blond wig, stuffed a sock down the front of her pants, and imitated Robert Plant while lip syncing to *Ramble On*." Lydia laughed when Sunny reached behind her and tried to pinch her.

Noel killed the engine. "I would've liked to have seen that."

Sunny shook her head and laughed. "That was a one-shot deal brought on by too much caffeine and sugar."

Lydia and Harper climbed out of the Jeep before the doors were even open and took off into the cemetery. Noel and Sunny got out, as well, and slowly ambled through the dilapidated wrought iron entrance. It was easy for some to assume the place was haunted because it was so rundown. An eerie-looking statue of an angel in the middle of the yard was mostly covered in vine except for part of its face and wings.

"Are we okay?" Sunny asked as she gazed up at it.

"Are you asking me or her?"

Sunny laughed as her gaze moved to Noel. "I haven't heard from you," she said as her smile faded.

"You were clear about us not seeing each other until today." Noel knelt and picked a wildflower with red spiky petals and handed it to Sunny. "I hope that's not poisonous."

"Oh, thanks!" Sunny chuckled. "You're so romantic, Noel, bringing me to a cemetery and giving me a poison flower."

"I don't want to be typical. Anyone can take you to dinner and a movie." Noel clasped her hands behind her back and began walking slowly toward the girls as they wandered deeper into the graveyard looking at the headstones.

Sunny moved alongside her. "This is a red spider lily. Ethan looked them up online when they came up all over the yard."

"Why didn't you call me?"

Sunny laid the flower atop one of the tombstones and said, "I didn't want to appear pushy."

Noel glanced at her. "Did you want to?"

Sunny was quiet for a second. "Yes, I did. This is kind of new for me. I...don't normally do this kind of thing."

"Why did you choose me?"

"I find you very attractive." Sunny stuffed her hands into her back pockets. "Harper mentioned that you don't do relationships." She sighed. "I haven't exactly been lucky in that department, to be honest. I've given up on having one. I still crave being in the arms of someone else, though."

Noel was surprised by the candor of Sunny's reply. "I'm not opposed to relationships, my last went for eight years. We weren't right for each other. I felt trapped, but at the same time, I did love her, and I guess I thought it would all work out. I'm supposed to be looking for another cat, but there aren't as many strays out there as you might think."

"You just lost me." Sunny stopped walking.

"There's this amazing love therapist that says people fall into two categories when it comes to relationships. There's the dog type that always wants to be by your side and needs your nonstop affection. The cat is equally loving, but they require space. I would say that the cat gets overwhelmed with too much attention, and the dog doesn't truly understand that the cat loves deeply, even though it's not up your butt and constantly nipping at your hand for a pet."

"All dogs aren't like that. I've had a couple, and they were very independent."

"I had a cat that slept on my neck anytime I lay down, so I'd have to agree that the theory is somewhat flawed. But you get the general gist."

Sunny nodded as they resumed walking. "Who is this crackpot therapist?"

"You've already met her, and she makes a mean roast."

Sunny's face colored. "Sorry about the crackpot comment."

"Don't be," Noel said with a smile. "She's often full of shit."

"I should've...I don't..." Sunny looked skyward. "Never mind."

"I do mind." Noel nudged Sunny playfully. "What were you going to say?"

"Are you afraid of diseases?"

Noel stopped walking, a tad offended and completely surprised. "You probably should've asked me that before you came over the other night."

"I had a little anxiety attack the next day because like I said, I don't normally do this kind of thing. And before we...my mind was solely on what I wanted, and I didn't stop and think to ask if you were safe," Sunny blurted out.

Noel gazed at her partially amused. "Are you always this blunt?"

"Shouldn't you be?"

"I don't go down on the women I sleep with, and they don't go down on me...normally."

Sunny's eyes widened. "But we did that."

Noel nodded and started walking again. "I lost my head. If it makes you feel better, I'm tested regularly. I know Harpy probably told you that I'm basically a slut, but that's not entirely true. I have had what I consider casual sex with...buddies—women who want the same thing."

Sunny caught up with her. "I'm sorry that I offended you. The look on your face said I did."

"I guess we shouldn't be too soft-skinned when making these kinds of arrangements. In this situation, it's good to be blunt."

They veered away from talking about their night together after that and caught up with the girls, who had decided to do some sort of ghost hunt with the cameras and voice recorders on their phones. Noel occasionally glanced at Sunny and found her staring at her with her mind seemingly a million miles away.

Pizza won the vote for lunch. Sunny and Noel sat side by side in a booth and watched the girls huddled together staring at Harper's phone and the pictures they'd taken at the cemetery in hopes of catching a ghost. Sunny rested her leg against Noel's and was pleased that she didn't pull away. To her, the contact at least meant that Noel had not decided to already end their arrangement because of the conversation at the cemetery.

"What is that?" Harper said suddenly.

"Your elbow."

Harper gazed at Lydia, their faces inches apart. "Why am in all of the pics you took?"

"Because it didn't make sense to just take pictures of woods and tombstones. You took a bunch of me, too."

"Yeah, look at this one." Harper tabbed through the pictures until she came to one that made them both laugh hysterically. She held the phone up for Noel and Sunny to see.

"Now that might be a ghost," Sunny said as she gazed at the half of Lydia's face when Harper had zoomed in on something.

Lydia sounded disappointed when she said, "That's the only one we caught then. I think after the hayride tonight, we should go back there and take some more."

Sunny tilted her head to the side with a sympathetic smile. "Aw, honey, you've lost your mind."

Lydia pointed at her. "And you're a chicken."

"We could stop at a hardware store and get an EMF detector. They're for electricians, but ghost hunters use them to detect energy fields," Harper said excitedly.

Noel laughed. "Did a ghost slip you a pocket full of cash to make this purchase?"

"No, but I'm hoping my aunt will," Harper said with a cheeky grin.

Noel shook her head with a sigh. "I'm having you drug-tested when we get home."

The pizza arrived before Harper could reply. Sunny picked up the serving tool and set a slice on Noel's plate first, Harper got one next, then Lydia. No one said anything for a few minutes as they devoured their lunch.

"Where do we go from here?" Sunny asked.

"There's a flea market close by. I don't think it's haunted, but is that something anyone would be interested in?" Noel asked.

"Totally." Lydia looked at Harper. "We might find an EMF detector there."

Harper nodded. "I'm in."

Sunny gazed at Noel. "I'm up for whatever."

"Do you need a porcelain Mardi Gras mask?" Sunny asked Noel as they stood at a booth.

"No, and I also don't need a standalone Batman toilet paper holder, but are you feeling the fake shrunken monkey heads?"

"I've already got a half-dozen, any more would just make it odd." Sunny picked up a wooden beaver with a bottle opener behind its teeth. "Think about it."

"I'm trying not to," Noel said as she moved to the next booth.

The girls were on the other end of the strip looking at a table full of tools. Sunny moved close to Noel, enjoying the way it felt when they brushed against each other. Even though what they had between them was only physical, there was a level of intimacy, as well. Sunny had been in Noel's arms, had tasted her kisses, and that was what she wanted then. She wondered if random acts of affection were part of the arrangement, but even if they had been, they still weren't free to do as they pleased. Aside from being surrounded by hundreds of people milling about, Lydia and Harper weren't far off.

Sunny didn't want to be faced with explaining to her daughter that she was not dating Noel, just sleeping with her.

She'd always tried to be a positive role model for Lydia, and she knew this would tarnish that. In addition, she was afraid of Inez. Noel might've been a big girl, but she was still Inez's baby, and as a mother, Sunny knew she would judge harshly any woman who wanted only one thing from her child.

Noel turned suddenly, wearing a mustache and beard. "Call me sexy."

"Oh, you are…or you were before the facial hair," Sunny said with a smile.

Noel removed the costume and laid it back on the table. "You have beautiful teeth."

"I'd think that compliment odd if it weren't coming from a dentist."

"You have a lovely smile in general," Noel said with sincerity.

"You make me do it often."

"Good," Noel said with a small nod and turned away. She seemed to be headed straight for the concession stand.

Sunny followed along. "What do you have your eye on?"

"You mostly, but the cotton candy is calling my name. I read somewhere that it has less sugar than a can of soda. Would you like to share with me or have your own bag?"

"I'll share, and I'll buy."

With the treat and two bottles of water, they found Lydia and Harper. "We're gonna go outside and enjoy our snack, y'all want anything?" Noel asked.

"The answer will be yes if we find an EMF detector," Harper said as she rifled through things at the booth she was standing in front of. "I'll text you."

"And I'll ignore it." Noel grinned when Harper scowled. "We'll be out back by the picnic tables."

Sunny pointed to a bench next to one of the exterior walls, and they took a seat. Noel held out a chunk of the candy. "First bite for me? I feel so honored," Sunny said as she plucked it from Noel's fingers.

"I know how to treat a lady." Noel dug some of the cotton candy out of the bag and hummed happily as she ate.

"So if my math is right, you had Lydia when you were twenty-four?"

"That's right. Looking at it in hindsight, though, I wished I would've waited until I was thirty. Personally, I think that's the right age to have children, you're wiser, more mature."

Noel fed Sunny another bite. "Was it hard?"

"Very. Ethan really came through for me then. My partner, Tamara, told me that she wanted kids the day we met. I saw it as some far-off dream, but we were together a couple of years when she wanted to make it a reality. She found a donor, and it didn't work out. She couldn't conceive. I didn't want to be pregnant, but she wanted a baby so desperately. I got pregnant on the first try."

"I assume you and Tamara broke up. Is she still in Lydia's life?"

Sunny waved off Noel's offer of more candy and stared at the water bottle. "One of the other reasons for waiting to have a baby is financial security. We were young and impulsive and so focused on having one that we really didn't consider how we were going to manage. Tamara and I ended up having to move back in with Ethan when Lydia was four, so we could catch up on the debt that we'd accumulated. When it seemed we were beginning to get our heads above water, Tamara's car died." Sunny released a sigh. "That's why she was with Ethan the day of the accident, he was taking her to work. She died on impact."

Noel put her hand atop Sunny's. "I'm at a loss for words. All I can say is that I'm so sorry."

"I had a child to take care of and Ethan. My own grief was shoved on a shelf somewhere, and I didn't revisit it until much later. Once I felt strong enough to venture back into the dating pool, I found it very disappointing, so I gave up."

"I apologize for making you talk about something that painful out here."

"You didn't force me." Sunny stared at the ground. "Lydia knows the general gist, but I've only ever really talked about it with Ethan. It's kind of freeing to explain it to you."

"I'll listen any time you want to talk."

Sunny gazed at Noel. "Thanks."

Chapter 13

As the sun began to set, they arrived at the cornfield where they would take the hayride. Noel bought all the tickets, despite Sunny's protests. Their departure was scheduled an hour out, and instead of standing in line, they wandered and ate pulled pork sandwiches, cheese fries, and whatever fattening thing they could get their hands on.

Sunny was sullen for a little while after their conversation about Tamara, but she began to slip back into a cheerful groove as they took their chances on a few of the games offered to those waiting for their hayrides. They tried unsuccessfully to silence a heckler in a dunking booth and failed at throwing beanbags into the mouth of a wooden pumpkin because the loud mouth continued to harass Noel.

"He called me a stick figure," Noel groused. "Am I really that skinny?"

"I think 'scarecrow in a ball cap' was more dead on," Harper said.

Sunny clamped her lips together tightly to keep from laughing at Harper's response. "Neither of those descriptions is true."

Noel didn't hear a thing as she watched a child pass with a caramel apple. "That is so bad for your teeth," she said as she pulled a twenty from her pocket and handed it to Harper. "Go get us all one, please."

Sunny watched Lydia and Harper go, then turned to Noel. "It's time for you to come out of the closet. You're a dentist with a sweet tooth, aren't you?"

"Every last one of my teeth is sweet," Noel said with a sigh.

"Why dentistry?"

Noel pointed at a kid running by. "When I was that age, I was horrified of the dentist. I think my mom would've muzzled me if she could. Dr. Lisbon was a great guy, and for some reason, he liked me. He told my mom that if I spent some time with him at the office, it might relieve my fears, so I became his honorary assistant one summer. He paid me five bucks a week, and his wife, who was the receptionist, made me a tiny lab coat, which I still have. When I wasn't with a patient, I spent my time with their son, William, in the playroom. Dr. Lisbon had ulterior motives when he made his offer, my real job was keeping Will out of his hair."

"Aw, how cute."

Noel jutted her chin. "Yes, I was adorable."

"I was talking about the coat," Sunny said with a laugh.

"You're a smartass, I like it."

"I interrupted, please continue."

"I squirted water and played with the suction, and I watched Dr. Lisbon work. He was right, it did take the fear out of it, but it also intrigued me. In high school, I worked as his receptionist. When I graduated dental school, I went right back to work for him. He's retired now, but Will and I work well together."

"Does your mother happen to have any pictures of you in that little lab coat?"

Noel nodded. "And I have the coat sealed in a plastic bag." She moved over to one of the straw bales and took a seat. "Now tell me something that will surprise me about your childhood."

"I was a cheerleader in high school."

Noel's jaw sagged. "Get out!"

Sunny nodded. "I can still do a split."

"I know," Noel whispered with a mischievous grin. "You've already demonstrated that you're very limber. Do a cheer!"

"Later."

Noel buffed her nails on the front of her shirt with flair. "I'm throwing a double dog dare on it."

Sunny looked at the crowd milling about, straightened her back, clenched her fists, and swung her arms. "Give me a C! Give me an—"

"No!" Lydia said in horror as she wrapped her arms around Sunny. "Mom, you promised never to do that in public again. It's embarrassing enough when Uncle Ethan wears your old uniform around the house."

Noel's eyes widened. "There's a uniform?"

Harper shook her head with a rueful expression as she handed Noel an apple. "Oh, you are so bad off."

Sunny joined Noel on the straw bale. "You got me in trouble."

"I never dreamed you'd actually do it."

"We wanna roll with Lydia's idea and go back to the cemetery after we leave here," Harper said.

Lydia nodded. "We think we have a better shot of catching a ghost on film in the dark."

"I can hardly wait," Sunny replied drolly.

Noel regarded Sunny as they settled into a wagon filled with straw and half a dozen other people with the insane desire to have the shit scared out of them. "Have you been on one of these hayrides before?"

Sunny shook her head. "I've never been to a haunted house, either."

"They like the people who get all freaked out, so when they come after you, just play it cool and they'll move to the next person."

"Got it, I'm cool." Sunny let out a screech that curled everyone's eyelashes when a guy dressed in a demon costume came up beside her.

"You may wanna work on your cool," Noel said nonchalantly.

After they endured a lecture about prohibited cellphone use and not jumping out of the ride, the tractor-drawn cart began to slowly move. Sunny sat as close to Noel as physically possible. She did her best to stare dispassionately at someone in a garish costume as he circled the wagon whipping everyone into a frenzy.

"Next time Harper and Lydia come up with a bright idea, I'm going to exercise veto power," Sunny whispered.

"You're gonna be..." Noel's eyes widened as she stared past Sunny. "That is one cool headless horseman."

Sunny's head whipped around just as the rider came charging out of the cornfield on a black horse. While all attention was focused on it, they were hit from the other side by a barrage of blood-covered creatures. Everyone in the cart screamed, and Sunny was the loudest.

Harper jumped right into Lydia's arms and stayed there. Noel didn't miss the supreme look of satisfaction on Lydia's face as she held Harper tight. She watched the pair curiously until hay started to fly around.

Sunny had completely lost her mind when the cart came to a crawl and they were surrounded by a group waving chainsaws. She was slinging hay and flopping around like a fish screaming at the top of her lungs. All of the cliché moments in the sappy romantic movies that Noel abhorred happened to her then. Sound faded as Sunny tried to bury herself beneath the hay laughing and yowling at the same time. *This is the woman I want*, Noel thought as she watched in amazement.

She'd done the unthinkable. Noel had always gotten aggravated with women who, after the proverbial roll in the hay, decided to let their heart enter the arrangement. She was finally guilty of the same, but as she stared at Sunny, she realized that she had done something much worse. She'd fallen under Sunny's spell at first sight.

Chapter 14

Lydia activated the voice recorder on her phone, hoping to catch the voices of the dead while she and Harper roamed the cemetery. Harper steadily snapped pictures while Noel and Sunny sat in the Jeep watching them. The flashes indicated their location; otherwise, it was pitch black in the shadows beneath the trees.

"No one I know would've been crazy enough to do this with me," Harper said with a laugh.

"If it's scary or stupid, I'm your girl."

"I bet your mom thinks we're insane."

"After what we just saw on the hayride, she has no room to judge."

Harper brushed against Lydia's arm. "Stay close to me, this is kinda creepy."

Lydia felt a rush of pride over being called upon as protector. "I got you," she said as she put her hand on Harper's back.

"Yeah, I think you do."

"Hey, I protected you on the hayride, didn't I?" Lydia flinched when Harper turned and faced her. Harper was so close she could feel her body heat and her breath on her face and neck. "What's wrong?"

"I think...you should kiss me."

Lydia had dreamed of this moment, certain that it would never happen. She wasn't sure if she'd really heard what Harper had just whispered. "What?"

Harper took a step back. "Look, it's okay if you don't want to. I shouldn't have—"

"No." Lydia reached blindly in the dark until she caught Harper's shirt. "I want to. I'm just surprised."

"Me too," Harper said, sounding nervous. She groaned when a chime sounded on her phone and the screen lit up. She snapped a picture, then stuffed the phone into her pocket. "Noel was freaking because she stopped seeing the flash."

Lydia was half blinded by the intrusion of light, but she still had a grip on Harper's shirt. Nerves had set in, and her hand shook slightly. She was compelled to ask Harper a bunch of questions but didn't want to do anything to ruin the moment. Harper moved close again, and Lydia took advantage of the opportunity. Harper's lips trembled against hers for a second, but Lydia felt a hand slip around the back of her neck. Emboldened, she deepened the kiss. Inside of her, it felt like New Year's Eve, mortar shells were exploding in her chest as their tongues met. Then the Jeep horn blared.

Harper pulled away with a groan. "I am gonna kill her. We should go, or she's going to come back here."

"Okay," Lydia said, dazed.

They walked in silence, and just before they reached the Jeep, Harper whispered, "That was the Fourth of July."

"Should we put the top back on?" Noel asked as she killed the engine to the Jeep in Sunny's driveway.

"No, it's going to be pretty tomorrow." Sunny glanced into the backseat where Lydia and Harper sat cuddled up together. "Did we freeze y'all?"

Both of them shook their heads to the contrary, but neither moved.

Noel got out and looked at them. "I think we did. This is the first time they've been still all day." She moved the front seat out of the way. "Harper," she said slowly. "You can get out now."

Lydia was the first to move and unclipped her seat belt. "You wanna do something tomor—"

"Yes, call me," Harper said as she tried to climb out with her seat belt still on.

Noel half dragged her out of the Jeep, gave her a little shake, then gazed at Sunny and Lydia. "We'd like to thank y'all for a fantastic day." She bumped Harper with her hip when she simply stood there staring at Lydia.

"It was a…great…really…great time. Thank you," Harper said, unable to peel her gaze off Lydia, who looked equally stupefied.

Sunny looked at both girls and gazed at Noel as her brow rose. "We had a wonderful time, too. Maybe we'll get together again soon?"

"I'd like that. Now I have to get my exhausted little statue home. Good night."

"I know you're about to say we need to talk," Harper said when they climbed into Noel's car. "But just give me some time to process, okay?"

All right, but when you come down to earth, we really need to have that chat." Noel smiled. "Put your seat belt on."

Sunny and Lydia still stood in the headlights of Noel's car as she backed out of the driveway. Sunny tugged on Lydia's sleeve. "What's going on with you?"

Lydia wasn't ready to talk about the kiss because she wasn't sure what it meant. "The ride home made me sleepy, it was a long day."

"That all?" Sunny asked as they walked to the back door.

"Uh-huh. You should probably shower first. You've got hay all in your hair."

Lydia showered as fast as she could, kissed Sunny and Ethan good night, then crawled into bed with her phone. She typed what seemed like fifty texts and erased them all until she decided on: *Why did u want me to kiss u?*

Harper's response was slow. *I like you a lot.* Another text followed immediately after the first. *More than a friend.*

Lydia covered her mouth when she released a squeal that sounded a lot like Ethan's. Her hands shook as she typed her reply. *I feel the same way. I have 4 a while. I was scared to tell u cause I thought u were str8.*

So did I, Harper replied.

"I knew I was a good kisser!" Lydia whispered and silently acknowledged that practicing on her arm was a good idea. Her thumbs were like lightning as she tapped on her screen. *Will you be my gf?*

Harper's prompt response was, *Yes.*

Can I come get u in the morn?

Yes, what time? Harper added a dancing emoji.

5…ok 10.

I'll be ready.

So the kiss was good?

Harper responded by loading up the screen with big-eyed emojis, then typed, *Awesome.*

I almost passed out when u asked me 2 kiss u.

I almost passed out when u did.

Lydia grinned. *Did u tell Noel?*

Not ready. Don't want lectures.

Lydia fully understood. That was the same reason she didn't tell Sunny anything, either, and feared that Harper sleeping over would end.

Our secret, Lydia typed back.

Have 2 go. Mom wants to hear bout today. Will text later. Harper included a heart.

Lydia sent her a screen full of them.

Chapter 15

"Meet me in the bush, I got coffee."

"Momma, it's six thirty," Noel whined into the phone. "I'm too tired for the bush."

"You weren't the other night. I saw Sunny's car. I didn't say anything when you were at the house because your father doesn't like to hear about you girls having sex. He just tells himself all you do is hold hands with your plentiful paramours."

Noel's eyes flashed open. "The spying has got to stop."

"Who's spying? I went outside to throw a peach at the cat yowling under my window. If you wanted it to be a secret, you should've had her park on the next block. Come to the bush, but go behind the house and sneak around the air conditioner so your father doesn't see you."

Noel flopped back into her bed. "You come here if you want to grill me."

"I like to smoke with my coffee. Noel, I ask so little, come to the bush."

Inez had played her first guilt card; Noel knew she'd deal out more until she got what she wanted. "I'll be down in a minute." She got up and slipped into a pair of cotton lounge pants and a hooded sweatshirt. She took the time to brush her teeth, all the while grumbling about living in proximity to her nosy mother. "I'm a grown woman. I pay my own bills, and still I have to answer to a five-foot, guilt-wielding shrimp."

Noel splashed water on her face, then pulled on her sneakers before she headed down the sidewalk. She wanted to charge right across the front yard to her mother's hiding place; instead, the dutiful daughter obeyed instruction. She was creeping past the back porch when the door opened and her father stepped out.

"What're you doing out here?" he asked with a glimmer of amusement in his eye.

Noel ran a hand through her hair. "I...couldn't sleep, so I came to see if Mom was making breakfast."

Joe leaned heavily against the porch railing. "No, she's hiding in her spy shrub. You think I'm dumb? You think I can't see the smoke rising up outta the foliage? You think I don't smell it?"

"If you know, why haven't you confronted her?"

"Because, if she knows that I know she's smoking again, she'll do it all the time." Joe tapped the side of his head. "I ain't stupid. She thinks I never noticed the bench we had out here disappeared. What else she got up in there?"

"It's gonna be the TV if you don't say something."

Joe shook his head. "I ain't worried about that, she knows I'll see the extension cord. You keep this between us."

Noel threw up her hands. "All right." She continued on behind the house once again grumbling. "She's keeping secrets, he's keeping secrets, Harper's got one, too. How the hell am I supposed to keep up with what I can't say?"

"What took you so long?" Inez handed Noel a travel cup as she joined her in the gardenia.

"There was a traffic jam by the bird feeder. Mom, you're killing me with this early morning stuff. I get two days out of the week when I can sleep in."

"I had three kids, you think I ever got a chance to sleep in? Cry me an ocean." Inez blew out a breath. "Noel, what are you doing?"

"I'm sitting in a bush drinking coffee at the crack of dawn."

"I mean with Sunny. She's a nice woman with a good head on her shoulders. This is someone you should be dating, not just pawing like an animal."

"Well, I'll tell you what, if you stop smoking, I'll ask her to marry me."

Inez contemplated the cigarette clutched between her fingers. "You're full of shit."

"You keep puffing on those things, and you may never get to see me married." Noel poked Inez in the arm. "You think about that."

"You think for a change instead of being ruled by what's in your pants."

"You don't have to lecture me, Momma, I had a moment. I think...Sunny might be my cat."

Inez's brusque manner vaporized, and her voice held hope as she asked, "Really?"

"It sounds silly, but I just feel like she's the one that's gonna snatch my heart away no matter how tightly I hold on to it. I can feel it slipping already, and I barely know her."

"You know what they say, fall in the fall, married by the spring."

Noel snatched a leaf off the bush. "I've never heard that."

"Well, I just made it up," Inez said with a shrug. "But it's true. You're gonna have to add onto your house because you've only got two bedrooms and you're gonna need more for Lydia and the uncle. Your yard's not that big, maybe you can go up instead of out. If I were you, while it was under construction, I'd have the bathroom redone. I love my big tub."

Noel stared at her with an incredulous expression. "I'm not that far along yet. You're giving me an anxiety attack."

"You're right." Inez took a drag off her cigarette and waved it as she said, "We should plan the wedding first, but in your case, it's gonna be a commitment ceremony, and since we don't have to have a church, we could do it in the backyard. I know your virgin boat has sailed, but I still want you to wear white because you look good in it, and it'll be spring and all."

Noel clutched her chest. "Would you stop?"

"What? I'm a planner. I look to the future, that's what I do. You'll make a good momma for Lydia because you've had so much practice with Harper and—"

"Say one more word, and I'm gonna start ripping limbs outta this bush. Your ass will be hanging out in the yard, and you'll be busted."

Inez's stare was menacing. "Don't threaten my bush, Noel." She quickly stuffed her cigarette into a bottle. "Hey, be quiet, there's DeVito," she whispered.

Noel watched the woman in her robe walk around on the patio and water the flowers. "Is she living there?"

"It appears so. I guess they found a perfect match in each other." Inez nodded. "Greg's a dog, and she…she's definitely a dog. That woman is butt ugly."

"You are so wrong for that."

Inez continued to watch DeVito's look-alike and whispered, "Fall in the fall, married by the spring."

"You think Greg's gonna marry her?"

"Yeah, but you ain't having a double wedding with those two."

"You're up early," Mary said as she walked into the kitchen. "Why are you already dressed?"

"Lydia and I are gonna hang out at her house today. She's got a project in English she's working on, and I'm gonna help."

Mary opened the fridge and pulled out the eggs. "Baby, you spent the whole day with her yesterday. Sunday is for family."

"I know, but she needs help. I'll be back in time for dinner at Nana's."

"Honey, I just really wish you'd stay—"

"What's the problem?" Harper exploded, feeling desperate to be alone with Lydia. "You never minded when I went places with Ashlynn on Sundays."

Mary whirled around. "Don't raise your voice with me."

"I'm sorry." Harper exhaled heavily as she noted the fire in her mother's eyes. "I slept bad last night, it's making me grumpy. I didn't mean to yell." She fidgeted and looked away from Mary's gaze. "It's just that I promised Lydia that I'd help her. She's depending on me, and she's already on the way to pick me up."

"Next time, ask me before you make plans. I'm still your mother."

Harper nodded. "Yes, ma'am." She looked at her phone when it chimed and saw Lydia's text message saying she was outside. "She's here. I'll be back for dinner, I promise." Harper walked over to Mary and gave her a hug. "I really am sorry about yelling."

Sunny's morning meditation was destroyed by Noel. Before she'd gotten started, Noel sent her a text invitation to meet for dinner later. Sunny eagerly accepted, then tried to get her inner focus aligned. When she tried to clear her mind, Noel pranced right on back in, holding cotton candy, staring back into Sunny's mind's eye with an *I know you want some* smirk on her face. And Sunny did, but it wasn't the candy she was interested in.

"Keep it simple, all sex," Sunny said as she opened her eyes to the foliage beyond the patio.

"Why?"

Sunny cleared her yoga mat by six inches and whirled around. "How'd you get out here without me hearing you?"

Ethan sat in one of the patio chairs with legs crossed and arms folded, a basket of fresh-cut flowers on the ground beside him. "I'm sorry. I was doing some gardening along the driveway and decided to take a break. I thought you heard me when I walked up. Let me help you with your internal debate."

"I find that I like her personality just as much as her physical attributes," Sunny said as she toyed with the corner of her mat, expecting a full-on *I told you so* rant and dance.

"I see, and how do you think she feels about you?"

Sunny frowned as she gazed up at Ethan. "What's wrong with you?"

"I want you to see me as your therapist," he said with a flourish of his hand.

"I see you as lunatic in a sun hat and pink housecoat."

"If it will help you open your mind, I will go inside and dress in a suit and tie."

"Don't go to all the effort, I'll still imagine you with the hat," Sunny said. "I think Noel likes me, too, or at least she's putting on one hell of a show. It's the way she looks at me and the things she says, and for the first time in a very long time, I'm touched by what I see instead of being repelled."

Ethan tapped his temple with his forefinger. "But her reputation gives you pause."

"Not as much as mine does," Sunny admitted. She wiggled her fingers. "I've got this wonderful tingly feeling going on, but I'm kind of nervous that it's temporary. It terrifies me that I might hurt her."

In a very officious tone, Ethan said, "In my experience, the tingly symptom is a very serious sign of infatuation, which leads to love if left untreated. My advice to you is to stop self-analyzing and enjoy the sensation."

"Oh, well, if that's your prescription, Doctor, I have no other choice but to take it," Sunny said angrily. "It's not that simple."

"Yes, it is," Ethan asserted. "I'm sure you see this developing fast, but it's been a long time coming. It's taken you years to fully heal. That you're afraid of hurting Noel means that you already care, and as you get to know her better, you're going to fall for her if you let yourself." He released a loud squeal. "I'm so excited for you!"

Harper pulled away from Lydia's kiss. Her eyes flew open wide as she asked, "Was that a dog?"

"No, it's Ethan on the patio."

"It makes me so nervous knowing they're close by," Harper said and moved farther away. "I like kissing you, though…a lot."

"When Mom leaves, we'll have some privacy because Ethan won't come in without knocking."

Harper's pulse skyrocketed as she gazed at Lydia. Her mind whirred with all sorts of exciting and nerve-wracking possibilities. She practically jumped out of her skin when Sunny knocked on the door and pushed it open.

"Hey girls, I'm about to—Harper, are you okay, honey?"

"Yes, ma'am."

Sunny stared at her for a moment. "Your face and neck are all red."

"The…uh…movie freaked me out."

Sunny glanced at the TV. "You're watching *Shrek*."

"Talking donkeys freak me out," Harper said as her blush deepened. "And I choked on a nut."

"O...kay," Sunny said and smiled. Lydia looked stupefied when Sunny turned her attention to her. "I'm going to take a shower, then run a few errands."

Lydia nodded. "Okay."

Sunny backed out of the room while Lydia and Harper stared at her like a couple of owls. She stood in the hall for a moment, brow furrowed, after she closed the door and went to find Ethan. He was in the salon trying to trap Tobi in a corner while waving a cat brush.

"Hey, do me a favor," Sunny said softly.

"You want me to do something with that mustache?"

"You're giving me a complex about that."

"I'm sorry, what do you need?"

"Check on the girls every now and then. I just went in there, and both of them looked like deer caught in headlights."

Ethan's brow rose. "What do you think they might be doing?"

"I don't know, but whatever it is, it was enough to put a deep blush on Harper's face."

Ethan pursed his lips. "Perhaps, Harper isn't straight?"

"I'm beginning to wonder."

Chapter 16

Noel sat up, and every hair on her head seemed to be pointing a different direction. "When I said dinner, this wasn't what I had in mind, but I'm not complaining," she said with a goofy grin.

Sunny sat up beside her. "I feel like I'm having an affair, sneaking off, going to a motel room. It's kind of exciting."

Noel gazed at her. "That's really what we're doing if you think about it, except we're hiding from children and nosy family instead of spouses. It's not entirely guilt-free. Harper is going to be upset when she finds out I didn't honor her request to leave you alone." She leaned over and kissed Sunny. "I blame you for being irresistible."

"I'm glad you think so." Sunny flopped back down and pulled Noel with her. "Noel, is Harper gay?"

"That seems to be the question on everyone's mind lately. Why do you ask?" Noel stretched out and propped her head in her hand.

"I felt like I may've interrupted something when I went to Lydia's room earlier today."

"They were alone in her room?" Noel asked with concern.

"Lydia told me Harper was straight, so I didn't think there was a need to restrict them to the living room."

"I'm trying hard not to betray Harper's confidence, but since it involves Lydia, I feel like you should know that Harper is questioning her sexuality right now."

"I think Lydia is thoroughly smitten with her, but don't worry, I have a man on the inside. Ethan is a genius at showing up at inopportune times."

"Good, that makes me feel better. They're kids, they've got a lot of hormones going, and I'd just hate to see them jump into sex right off the bat." Noel raised a finger and closed her eyes. "I'm a hypocrite."

Sunny covered her body with the sheet. "It is hard to argue that point at the moment since we are naked in bed together."

"We're grown women, though."

"How will Mary handle the news?"

Noel traced Sunny's lips with her fingertip. "I thought I knew, but I'm not sure now. She has her suspicions because she came over this morning and asked me if Harper had said anything. I think she's worried that the same thing that happened to me when I came out will happen to Harper."

"What did happen?"

"My best friend in high school, Julie, who was also gay, outed me. She didn't do it out of spite. She was in love with another classmate, who was dealing with her own sexuality struggles. Julie was trying to make her more comfortable and told her about me. Charlene turned right around and told someone else, and word spread. I wasn't ready for everyone to know, so I denied it when people began asking questions, but no one believed me. I was on the track team, and so was my arch nemesis, and she had a field day with the news. One day in the locker room, she and two other girls decided that I shouldn't be allowed to dress for P.E. or for track meets with them. They took all my stuff and tossed it into a storage closet. I didn't take the high road, so to speak. I was furious, and I provoked Monica until she hit me, so I could say she threw the first punch. We tied into it, and her friends jumped in. No one came to my aid, not even our coach, and I basically got my ass kicked by the three of them."

Sunny took Noel's hand and kissed it. "People can be cruel. I empathize with Mary's concerns, and I'm sorry for what happened to you."

"I think what happened to you was worse. Lydia kind of let it out of the bag that you and Ethan were disowned."

"Pretty much," Sunny said dispassionately. "We Chases are a very stubborn lot. My sisters have reached out to me, but I'm not ready to let go of how they participated in the estrangement for years. I knew what my parents would do if they found out, but I was blown away when my siblings stood with them. What really hurt was that my sisters and I always kept in touch with Ethan after he and Dad stopped speaking, but they cut me off. They've apologized since, and I've forgiven, but I'm just not willing to let them in again."

"I can understand that."

"I did tell my younger sister Deidra that I have a daughter, and I'm sure she probably told Mom and Dad. Neither has made any attempt to contact me or even ask about Lydia. I also told her about what happened to Ethan, but none of them called or sent flowers, not even a card." Sunny blew out a breath. "My anger flares up, and I have to remind myself that I pity them. What little love they possess has serious limitations, and in my opinion, that's not really love at all."

Dressed in the loudest pair of clunky shoes he owned, Ethan stomped down the hall to Lydia's bedroom, pounded on the door, and sang, "I made cookies."

He was about to pound again when Lydia said, "Great."

Ethan pushed the door open and strode in with a platter in his hand and noticed that both of the girls' faces were flushed and their lips bruised. Harper didn't make eye contact, and Lydia fidgeted. The bed where Lydia sat was rumpled, and Harper was across the room in a beanbag chair where she couldn't see the TV.

"There's nothing like fresh-baked cookies to go with a movie marathon," Ethan said as he placed the tray on the corner of Lydia's desk. "Oh, *Pretty In Pink*, that's a classic. I absolutely loved the eighties, the big hair, and the crazy colors of the clothing." He sighed and fanned his face like a beauty queen who had just been crowned. "The music, oh, how I danced."

"That's so cool, and thanks for the cookies." Lydia stared at Ethan, silently imploring him to leave.

"I think y'all should watch *The Breakfast Club* next." Ethan waved a hand. "Keep that whole Molly Ringwald vibe going. I've always thought she was precious with those pouty lips, that red hair, and cherubic face. Oh, Harper, with just a little makeup and a wig, I could make you look just like her."

"That would be fun sometime, but—"

"Yay!" Ethan grabbed her by the arm and practically yanked her out of the chair. "Your skin tone is perfect. Lydia, get Tobi, she went under your bed, and she's been shitting in shoes lately."

"I should've taken you to a better hotel," Noel said sadly as she picked mushrooms off the slice of pizza she held and placed it in Sunny's mouth. "I'm so disappointed about the absence of room service."

"You should've told me that you didn't like shrooms," Sunny said as she chewed.

"You didn't say anything about the sausage, so we're even. What other foods do you dislike?"

"I'll eat just about anything but fennel."

"I love it," Noel said with a smile. "I hate turkey."

Sunny was about to take a bite and stopped. "Noel, that's un-American."

"Mom says the same thing, but it's got an odd taste I can't stand no matter how it's prepared."

Sunny wrinkled her nose. "I hate those little marshmallow chicks they sell around Easter."

"I smear peanut butter on a cracker, stick the chick on it, then add another cracker and nuke it in the microwave for a few seconds."

"You really are a sugar addict."

Noel laughed. "I am. Mary hates that about me because if she even looks at something sweet, she gains weight," she said, and her smile faded. "She's one that's had it kind of hard, too. She married what we all thought was a fantastic guy. She was so happy living the life she always wanted. They had Harper and built a beautiful house. Then all of the sudden, David started to change. He began working all the time, and everyone thought he was just trying to keep their heads above water. The truth was, he was embezzling what amounted to almost a million dollars, and he had like five mistresses. Mary lost everything but Harper."

"Was he arrested?"

"Oh, yeah," Noel said with a nod. "He's sitting in a federal pen right now. Harper won't have anything to do with him, but Mary fears that when he gets out, he'll try to mend that relationship, and she doesn't trust him."

"We both have our share of family drama, don't we?"

"Every family does, some are just better at keeping it hidden. Let's get off that topic." Noel wiped her hands on a napkin and took a sip of her soda. "Do you like dancing?"

Sunny shook her head. "I can't dance. It's a phobia. I'll goof off around the house with Ethan and Lydia but no way in public. I just freeze. I can't move, and I really don't know why. What's your hang-up?"

"You're gonna laugh, and it's okay if you do, but I will not go to a bowling alley."

Sunny nodded. "It's the shoes, right?"

"Let me just say that in one night, I passed the foul line and watched as my feet flew up in front of my face. As I was helped off the floor, someone dropped a ball on my foot. I have not been back since."

Sunny gazed at Noel for a moment. "I'm not going to laugh."

"When I did that somersault, I ripped the crotch out of my pants."

"Okay, I'm going to smile."

"I hadn't done laundry, so I was wearing the oldest pair of underwear I owned covered in unicorns."

Sunny covered her mouth. "You're making this so hard."

"There was a hole right in the ass. The unicorns were gathered around it as though they were looking in."

Sunny snorted. "Okay, you win."

"Mountains or beach?"

"Mountains," Sunny said with a nod.

Noel grimaced. "I'm beach."

"I like it, too, but I prefer the mountains in the fall when the leaves are turning."

Noel smiled. "Dark chocolate or milk?"

"Dark."

"I'm a milk chocolate lover. We appear to be opposites on a few things."

"Is that disappointing?" Sunny asked seriously.

"They're little things, but I feel that maybe we should re-evaluate our arrangement."

Sunny steeled herself, thinking that maybe she'd assumed too much about Noel, whose expression was very serious.

"I like you," Noel began tentatively, then chewed at her bottom lip. "To be honest, I didn't particularly want to enter into this no strings arrangement. I wanted to date you, Sunny. Given your history, I know that's probably something you don't want to hear, but if we keep going like this, I'm just gonna want more. If you want to continue on strictly sexual, I'm…I'm going to have to back out."

"You want to date me," Sunny said, needing the clarification.

Noel nodded. "I think we have more between us that needs to be explored."

"I agree." Sunny ran her finger along Noel's jaw. "And I'd like to see where this leads. We both have histories that are kind of alarming, though."

"Maybe it's naïve, but we both had our own reasons for our unwillingness to commit, and I think that's why we understand each other."

"No, I don't. Why didn't you want to be in a relationship?"

"For a long time, I guess I was in love with the idea of being in love. I got into relationships with women hoping that the feelings I'd dreamed about would magically appear. The last was with Brenna. The first few years were good, we had things in common, the newness of the relationship kept it exciting. I bought the house, and she moved in with me. I woke up one day with the realization that I wasn't in love with her, but I stayed because I did care for her. I couldn't stop the divide that began to gradually form between us, and we just became like roommates with a commitment. I felt trapped, and eventually, she left. Like you admitted that day at the cemetery, I wanted someone to hold, but I wasn't ready to try for anything substantial again."

"What makes this different?"

Noel looked away. "You may not like the answer, which is I don't know. All I can say is that I feel something that I've never felt before, and I want to hold on to it as tight as I can. I feel like I'm part of something special when I'm with you," Noel said, borrowing Harper's line because that simply summed it up.

Sunny nodded as she took it all in. "Okay. I'll take this journey with you. If we're lucky, it'll last a lifetime."

Lydia touched the side of Harper's face. "I'm so sorry, baby."

Harper pulled the visor down and looked at herself in the mirror. She'd left the wig behind, but her face was so made up she looked like a Raggedy Ann doll. She and Lydia had practically run out of the house when Ethan dug into his closet for an eighties outfit for her to model. She decided that the indignity was worth the pleasure of making out with Lydia. Had Ethan not interrupted, she would've done something she wasn't sure she was ready for. It wasn't that she didn't want to, but the idea of being caught with her pants down, literally, was terrifying because getting in trouble might infringe on what she considered precious time with Lydia.

"What's wrong?" Lydia asked.

"Nothing. I was just thinking about being alone with you."

"Come spend the night with me again. We'll sleep in my bedroom this time." Lydia licked her lips nervously. "If you want to."

Harper smiled at her. "I do. My mom won't let me stay over during the week, though."

"We're off Tuesday for teacher training day, remember?"

Harper's heavily made-up eyes flew open wide. "I'd forgotten about that." She squeezed Lydia's hand and looked out the window at the kids playing on the swings in the park. "You're gonna have to take me home soon. Will you stay for dinner?"

"Yeah, I'll take any minute I can spend with you."

"Looking like this?" Harper asked with a laugh.

"I still think you're beautiful," Lydia said seriously. "I always have." She put a finger under Harper's chin and turned her face toward her. "The first time I saw you was in the hall outside the library at school. I didn't get into trouble, and Mrs. Talbot didn't make me paint the badger. I told you that because I wanted an excuse to be around you. I've been crazy about you since the first day I saw you."

Harper was stunned. "Seriously?"

Lydia nodded as she met her gaze.

"Why?"

"You *are* beautiful, Harper. I don't understand how you don't know that."

Harper swallowed hard. "Kiss me."

"Someone might see," Lydia said as she looked around.

"I don't care." Harper climbed halfway across the seat, clasped Lydia's face in her hands, and kissed her with all she had.

Chapter 17

When they parked in front of the Savinos' house, Corey was on the porch talking on her phone. Lydia gazed at her for a moment. "You're prettier than your cousin."

"Look at her closely. She's got a tiny waist and big boobs and…you know what, don't look at her."

Lydia turned to Harper. "I could never look at her the way I do you. I mean that with all my heart."

"Oh, my God, you're so cute," Harper said with a groan. "You're making me love you."

"I hope so because I—"

They both nearly leapt out of their seats when Corey banged on Harper's window. "Y'all gonna sit in there all day? What the fuck happened to your face?"

Harper shoved her out of the way with the door when she opened it. "It was part of a costume, shut up."

"You need to hurry up. We're all waiting on you so Nana will let us eat." Corey looked at Lydia as she walked around the front of the truck. "How come you're not dressed up?"

"Because we were working on Harper's costume."

Corey threw a hand on her hip as she returned her attention to Harper. "What are you supposed to be?"

"Molly Ringwald, we're bringing the eighties back."

Corey shot Lydia a look. "I suppose you're gonna be that dork in *Pretty in Pink*, Ducky. You're too cute for that. I think you should be Andrew McCarthy's character." Corey recoiled at the scowl on Harper's face. "What? It was meant as a compliment."

"Just. Go. Away," Harper said slowly.

"Wow, you're being a total bitch tonight." Corey threw up her hands and marched off.

When Harper and Lydia walked into the house, Harper decided to forgo any more questions and announced, "The makeup on my face is practice for my Halloween costume. I'm Molly Ringwald, and now, I'm going to the bathroom to wash it off."

Heads poked around the wall between the kitchen and living room. "Oh, the eighties, I love it!" Mary exclaimed. "You've nailed the look, all you need are the clothes and a curly red wig."

"What's a Molly Ringballed?" Joe asked as he got up from his recliner.

"Wash later, you look gorgeous. We eat now," Inez said. "Lydia, I'm glad you're joining us. You can have Noel's spot since I don't know where she is."

"Thanks for having me," Lydia said shyly when she noticed the dark look on Mary's face.

Joe said the blessing and asked for the Lord's intervention once again in the Saints game. Inez spoke the family oath, everyone toasted, and plates began being passed around. Inez pointed at Lydia. "Have you met Harper's Uncle Matt and his wife, Lauren?"

"No, ma'am."

"She's polite, this one." Inez turned her attention to Matthew and Lauren. "This is Lydia Chase, our new friend. Her mother had dinner with us last week, but you missed her."

"It's nice to meet you," Matthew said kindly. "Do you go to school with Harper?"

"Yes, sir."

"Then you probably already know Corey and Mason, too," Lauren added.

"Yes, ma'am." Lydia smiled at the siblings, who sat side by side.

"So what did you two get into today?" Mary asked as she passed the bread to Corey.

Harper discreetly poked Lydia's leg with her finger, hoping she would run with the lie as she said, "We finished the project

Lydia was working on for school. Then we just hung out and watched movies and ate the cookies that Ethan made for us."

"Well, why didn't you invite Sunny to dinner, as well?" Mary asked.

"She was out running some errands," Lydia offered.

"That might explain why you couldn't reach Noel on her phone," Matt said with a laugh.

Inez narrowed her eyes at him, and he quickly sobered.

"I wanna take a vote." Joe pointed his fork at Lydia. "You weigh in on this, too. Who thinks the porch would look great painted black and the railing painted gold?"

No one raised a hand but Lydia.

Lauren shook her head. "Dad, it won't match the rest of the house, it's white."

"Black and gold match white, it's on my Saints jersey, and it looks great." Joe shrugged. "I think it'd look good. I already bought the paint."

Matthew grinned at him. "Oh, man, you wanna die, don't you?"

Sunny laughed as Noel twirled her and pulled her back close. "You're light on your feet," Noel said against her ear. "I'll even bowl if we can use tennis balls."

"Do you still have the unicorn underwear?"

Noel laughed as she held Sunny tight. "That's a new phobia. I always make sure I throw out old pairs just in case I rip my pants again."

"This has been a delightful date," Sunny said as she laid her head on Noel's shoulder.

Noel grinned. "I swear that one day I'll take you on a real one." Music played softly from the clock radio beside the bed, and moonlight streamed through the slats of the shuttered window. Sunny felt perfect in her arms, and it stunned Noel to realize she would've been content to sway with her all night.

"I have to go," Sunny said and placed a kiss on Noel's neck. She laughed when Noel danced her away from the door.

"When will I see you again?"

"I have a training meeting Monday and Tuesday evening. We try to schedule them between day and night shifts with the plant staff. I need to go grocery shopping Tuesday since I was busy this weekend. How about Wednesday? Would you like to have dinner then?"

"Yes, and just so you know, I check my phone between patients in case you want to send me a text that says something extremely naughty or sweet. Either will be gladly accepted."

Sunny clasped Noel's face and kissed her again. "I'll remember that. You have to let me go now."

Noel sighed as she reluctantly released her. "Text me, so I know you're home safe."

Sunny stole one more kiss. "I will."

When Noel got home, her headlights illuminated Harper where she sat on the swing. "What're you doing here so late? What's wrong?" Noel jumped out of her car and noticed that all the lights to the garage apartment were off. "Does your mom know you're here?"

"No, I sneaked out because I needed to talk to you. I've been sitting on your swing freezing my ass off waiting for you."

"Harper," Nocl exclaimed. "You don't sneak out!" She unlocked her back door and pulled her inside.

"It's not like I'm going to a club, and besides, your house is three doors down." Harper grasped the front of Noel's shirt. "I'm falling in love, and I'm totally freaking out. I am gay. I'm sure of it now. Lydia makes me feel like I'm floating, and I can't stand to be apart from her. She's so sweet, and I have never felt like this about anyone. I've never thought that much about sex, but I do now, all the time." Noel blinked as Harper continued to hit her with a barrage of information. "I want her. I've never *wanted* anyone, not like this. And now I understand why. I'm gay, a lesbian. This is why no one excited me before. I could kiss her forever."

"I'm excited for you, I really am." Noel led Harper to a chair and sat her down. "But just the other day, you told me you thought you *might* be gay. Can you sit back and consider how fast all of this is going?"

"What? You think I'm not gay?"

"I think you're moving way too fast," Noel said as she sat, thinking more about Harper saying she wanted to have sex with Lydia.

"I can't stop my feelings. I'm falling for her, and she loves me."

"You don't know her," Noel said emphatically. "What you're feeling right now is infatuation and lust. You've got to get a grip, Harper. You're not acting like yourself. You aren't impulsive, you don't sneak out of the house, and normally, you don't snap at your mother."

Harper's brow shot up. "You talked to her? To Mom?"

"She came over here and asked me if I knew what was up with you. I didn't tell her anything. That was really hard because she's my sister. She loves you more than anything else in the world. I think you should tell her what's going on with you."

"Not yet." Harper shook her head. "I'm not ready. She won't let me spend the night at Lydia's if she knows."

"And you shouldn't. Standard dating rules apply even to Lydia."

Harper's jaw sagged. "I didn't expect to hear that from you. It's not like I'm gonna get pregnant. What're you worried about?"

Noel sounded just like Inez when she spat out, "What I said, you're going too fast." Noel's phone chimed with Sunny's text. "Give me a sec, I have to answer this."

Harper waited until Noel typed out her response and stared into her eyes. "That was Sunny, wasn't it? You were with her tonight, that's why you weren't at dinner."

"I like her a lot. We've talked…she knows my history, and I know hers, we're going to date."

"I told you not to," Harper snapped.

"I don't have to have your permission, but I would like your understanding."

"You aren't being very supportive of my feelings, but you want me to understand?"

"I want you to think, baby. The other day, you weren't sure you were gay, now you are, and you're telling me you want to have sex with Lydia." Noel held up a finger when Harper's mouth popped open. "I know that's hard to hear coming from me. All I'm asking here is that you slow down."

Harper scowled as she stood. "The reason I always talk to you is because you never make me feel like a kid, but you did just now."

"I'm not trying to belittle you. Please, sit back down."

"No! I'm going home. Thanks a lot."

Noel stood and gave Harper a few-second lead before she followed, wanting to make sure that Harper made it back inside safely. Like a stalker, she hid behind bushes as she trailed Harper to the apartment and watched from the shadows as she slipped back inside. Two cats howled somewhere near her parents' house, and Noel stayed hidden as the front door opened. Inez stepped out and threw something in the direction of the ruckus. When she went back inside, Noel made her trek home feeling terribly conflicted. She'd just basically lectured Harper about things she herself was doing. She barely knew Sunny, and already she was behaving like a love-struck puppy with the sex drive of a rabbit.

Chapter 18

Monday was difficult for Noel. Her mind went from Sunny and the quickly evolving feelings she had for her. Then it wandered to Harper, and she debated how to correctly handle that situation. She wasn't comfortable being in the parental role in this case. She felt Mary should be the one setting the guidelines for what Harper could and could not do. By the time she got home that evening, she had a headache, and she realized it was going to get worse when she pulled into the driveway.

Inez was perched on Noel's patio swing, a cigarette in her hand and several bottles of booze near her feet. "Momma, what's going on?" Noel frowned at her burn pit being used as a giant ashtray.

"I went shopping today," Inez began dismally. "While I was out, Greg found my bush when he was working in the yard. He and your brilliant father decided that it was a hideout for a stalker or vagrant, so they trimmed the hedge down to nothing. So I went back to the store and stocked up on supplies. The wooden fence around your yard makes a great hiding place, but there's not a damn thing to watch back here but squirrels."

What little privacy Noel had enjoyed was gone. "I've got an azalea hedge out front. The guy on the other side of me likes to wash his car in a Speedo."

Inez waved her off. "Those things make me itch, they got something on the leaves." She clutched her chest as she said, "I'm heartbroken."

"So am I," Noel said sincerely. "Have you considered just quitting the smoking? Then you could sit anywhere."

"I don't wanna sit just anywhere," Inez spat out. "That bush was my secret place, and I had a good view. It was a no-dog zone...well, except for the Martins' poodle. He pissed on the bush a lot. Still, it was better than your canine father in my business all day long." She sighed. "I'm so depressed I didn't cook tonight, and it's just as well, Mary has plans, Harper's staying at Lydia's, and your father—"

That horny little fart, Noel thought and kept her tone neutral as she said, "I thought that wasn't allowed on school nights."

"They're off tomorrow for some teacher thing. Hey, where were you last night?"

Noel took a seat beside Inez on the swing. "I was with Sunny."

"Why didn't you bring her to dinner?"

"We wanted some time alone."

Inez's frown deepened. "You know how important it is to me to have all my kids over for dinner at least one night."

"Will I ever be a master of guilt, even though I've never given birth?" Noel asked with a sigh.

"Sorry but no. It's a consolation gift from God after your body is stretched out, your feet don't fit in your shoes anymore, and you got a baby on your lap shitting all over your last clean dress. Oddly after that stops, all you want is your children to be close."

Noel scrubbed her hands together. "I'll be at next Sunday's dinner."

"Did you have a nice time?"

"I asked her out, we're gonna actually date. She likes me, I like her, we're gonna see where it goes."

"I already know where it's gonna go." Inez patted Noel's cheek. "I got mother's intuition, another gift from God."

Sunny got out of her meeting at eight and checked her phone. The text message from Noel read: *Please call me on your way home, I need to discuss something with you.* Sunny felt a tingle of foreboding as she climbed into her Jeep and sat there for a moment. She realized that she was genuinely frightened that Noel might be having second thoughts. Her finger shook slightly as she opened her address book and pressed Noel's number.

"We have a problem," Noel said by way of greeting.

Sunny surprised herself when she said, "Let's work it out."

"Bottom line, Harper thinks she's in love with Lydia, and she's ready to explore her sexual urges. And she's sleeping over at your house tonight. Here's where it gets really sticky for me. My sister doesn't know any of this, and when she finds out that I was aware of Harper's desires and knew that she was spending the night with Lydia, she is gonna to want to kill me."

"I'm so not cool with this." Sunny turned the engine to her Jeep and switched the call to hands-free. "Kids usually find a way to do what they want to do, but that doesn't mean we're supposed to provide the place for them to do it and turn a blind eye."

"This is a struggle for me. I suppose if they were both eighteen, I might feel a little differently."

"Why don't you meet me at the house, and we'll talk to them together?" Sunny suggested.

"How long will it take you to get there?"

"About thirty minutes."

"I'll be there then." Noel cleared her throat. "I'm sorry to just throw all of this on you. I'm sure after a long day this is the last thing you want to deal with."

Sunny smiled. "You're right, but the high side is that I'll get to see you."

"It makes me happy that you're happy about the prospect of seeing me, and I'm happy that I have a chance to see you. I'm working with a theme here, did you catch it?"

"You're...happy?"

"Ecstatic, I walked on a little cloud all day. I'm gonna take a quick shower and head your way."

"I'll be there on my own cloud."

Noel walked over to Sunny's Jeep and opened her door. "How was your day, honey?" she asked with a smile as she took Sunny's hand and helped her out.

"Long and drawn out." Sunny wrapped her arms around Noel's waist and kissed her. "That made it better. You smell nice."

"Oh, don't nuzzle me," Noel said with a groan. "I'll kidnap you, I swear I will. Wait, is Sunny a nickname?"

"Ethan gave it to me. My given name is Susan Ellice after my grandmother. I started answering to Sunny when I was nine and nothing else."

"I'm Ruth Noel Savino. My parents have a whole Bible theme going. Mary, Matthew, but Mom's favorite holiday is Christmas, so I've been Noel since birth."

"Ethan's first name is Myron," Sunny whispered. "If you ever really want to piss him off, call him that."

When they walked inside, Ethan greeted them wearing a red flannel shirt that he'd cut the sleeves off, a pair of jeans, and a baseball cap. He held out his arms. "I went butch. What do y'all think?"

Sunny glared at him. "Those are my jeans, aren't they?"

"They probably got into my things by mistake," he said, avoiding her gaze. "It's good to see you, Noel."

"Great to see you. I like the butch look on you."

He smiled and kissed her cheek. "You know how to make a gay man feel good."

Sunny looked into the living room and turned to Ethan. "Where are the girls?"

"They're watching a movie in Lydia's room. I've been in there a million times, and I think Lydia is pissed at me because she threw something at the door after my last visit."

"Did Lydia ask your permission to have overnight company?" Sunny asked.

"She told me you were okay with it. That's exactly how she said it, 'Mom's okay with it.' She didn't talk to you?" Ethan looked as though he was the one in trouble.

"No, she didn't." Sunny took Noel's hand. "We're going to have a chat with them."

"Oh, my," Ethan said as he watched them go.

The girls were seated side by side in Lydia's beanbag chairs when Sunny and Harper entered the room. The expression on Harper's face when she saw Noel went from shock to anger to resignation in a matter of seconds. Lydia played it cool. "Hey, Mom, Harper's gonna stay with us tonight. What're y'all up to?"

Sunny led Noel over to the bed where they both sat down. "I'm not going to mince words. We know that you two have a mutual adoration for each other."

Harper looked away when Noel caught her eye.

"You're both still living at home," Sunny continued. "You still have to abide by rules. You're dating and that's great, but y'all are not going to have sex under this roof. Harper, I don't know your mother very well, but I'm sure she'd be upset if I allowed that to happen." Sunny set her gaze on Lydia. "And you know I would not allow it."

"Thanks for keeping your promise," Harper said snidely and glared at Noel.

"I haven't told anyone but Sunny because you forced my hand. We're here to have a conversation. If you're going to cop an attitude, we'll leave right now," Noel said firmly.

"We've been talking, too, and it's not like y'all have to worry that either of us will get pregnant." Lydia shrugged. "We care about each other, I don't understand why it's a big deal."

"Well, you're seventeen and not technically adults," Sunny said and looked to Noel for help.

"Wait, if we're eighteen, it's okay for us to have sex then?" Harper asked.

Noel jumped into the fray. "What we're trying to tell you is this is all too soon. And yeah, we'd like for you to wait until you're at least eighteen."

"I turn eighteen next month on the eighth," Lydia said with a smile.

"Until you're both eighteen," Noel quickly amended.

"Look, you only really just met and—"

"Don't go there," Noel whispered against Sunny's ear.

Sunny smiled at Lydia and Harper. "Give us just a moment, please." She took Noel by the hand and closed the door when they were in the hall.

"They're mopping the floor with us," Noel whispered.

"This isn't how I saw this going, that's for sure. I don't play the 'because I said so' card. I think kids should understand why we say no on certain things." Sunny bit her lip. "How do we argue this?"

"Noel's right, you're really getting your asses whacked in there."

The door on the linen closet next to Lydia's bedroom was slightly ajar. Sunny yanked it open, and Ethan grinned sheepishly. "Do you have advice, Mr. Eavesdropper?"

"All you've got left is to tell them their shit is going to burst into flames if they do it."

Sunny closed the door on him and gazed at Noel. "I think the only defense we have here is to tell them they can't do it in the house, and they have to be eighteen."

Noel nodded and sighed with resignation. "Okay."

When Sunny opened the door to Lydia's room, Lydia said, "We have more questions."

"Aw, shit," Noel whispered as she followed Sunny in.

"Okay, we know y'all are doing it already, so what's the difference here?" Lydia asked.

"And what makes you think we're doing *it*?" Noel said with an angry stare at Harper.

"Mom, you sneaked out the other night, I was in the bathroom when you came in with your hair all messed up." Lydia folded her arms. "You looked like you did it."

Sunny reclaimed her seat on the bed and pulled Noel down with her. "Noel and I are adults, the decisions we make are on us, but the ones y'all make are on us, too. Well…in your case, Harper, they're on Noel and your mother. In all fairness, she should've been in on this conversation."

Harper sank lower in her seat and covered her face with one hand.

"Sex is an important aspect to a relationship, you really shouldn't take it lightly if you have feelings for someone," Noel began. "If you go into it too soon, it clouds your judgment, it makes you overlook things that maybe you shouldn't. If you really do care for each other, at least wait until you're both eighteen. By that time, maybe your relationship will be on a more solid foundation, or y'all may decide you're better off as friends."

"I can't believe you're saying that," Harper said incredulously. "Every time Nana sees a different car in your driveway, she says, 'Oh, look, the coochie catcher is at it again.' How can you sit there and tell us to wait? You never do."

Sunny turned to Noel. "How many cars have you had?"

Noel shook her head, eyes wide. "I didn't get into all of them."

"And you had a threesome, that's how I got here. That's like so kinky, Mom," Lydia said.

"A threesome!" Sunny shouted. "Who on earth told you that?"

The door to the bedroom swung open, and Ethan ran in with a hand up. "She was nine and wanted to know about the mechanics. I couldn't bring myself to tell her that you shoved a turkey baster up your chuita. I freaked, that was the best I could come up with on the fly."

"And you thought a threesome was a better explanation? Why didn't you just ask me?" Sunny asked miserably as she gazed at Lydia.

"I did, and you started sputtering about bees. You got all nervous, it made me all nervous, and I just didn't want to talk to you about it anymore."

"Coochie catcher!" Noel scrubbed a hand through her hair. "I cannot believe her." She pointed at Harper. "And hey, thanks for that dig."

All four women started arguing until Ethan released a high-pitched scream that silenced them. "Now listen to the one who isn't having sex with anyone! None of y'all should be doing it right now." He clasped his hands against his chest and looked at the girls imploringly. "This is the sweetest time of your life. There's nothing like first love, and that's where y'all are headed. Take your time and savor every precious moment because this only happens once. The ideal, the hope is that you'll always be together, but in reality, so few high school sweethearts ever last the test of time." Ethan shook his head sadly. "The magic fades with every relationship after. You're wiser each time, you can no longer look at love with the wild-eyed innocence you have now. I'm sure in your minds you're thinking, 'Bullshit, he doesn't know how I feel,' but I do."

Ethan leaned against the wall. "I have one good hand, and I'd give it if I could just go back and spend one day where you are right now. No matter how tightly we hold on, everything changes. College, work, life will soon invade your sweet little sanctuary. Your only hope of surviving it as a couple is building a strong foundation, just like Noel said, and you can't make bricks out of hormones."

Lydia leaned close to Harper. "Did any of that make sense to you?"

"He's basically saying we shouldn't do it."

Ethan pointed at Noel and Sunny. "Learn from their mistake. They're both so jaded by life that they tried to just grab the cream off the top of something that can be wonderful. Fear of getting hurt again has made them act like two idiots in the past. Harper, that's the real reason your aunt has been catching coochies. Don't be so hard on her. Okay, I'm leaving now." Ethan backed out of the room to escape the looks that Noel and Sunny were giving him.

They all sat in silence for a moment, and Sunny said, "That was an interesting interjection."

Noel shrugged. "I'm going to give him an A for dramatic timing. You did it with a turkey baster?"

Sunny winced. "That's a conversation for another time."

"I still think we're ready for the cream," Harper said resolutely.

Noel frowned at her. "That's why you're going home with me tonight."

"Now that we're alone, feel free to explode."

Harper turned away from the passenger's window and scowled at Noel. "I've never been so humiliated in my entire life! Why did you have to make this such a big deal? People have sex all the time—*you* have sex all the time!"

Noel nodded with a sigh. "If I were in your shoes, that would've been my response, too."

"Well, that pisses me off even more. Why did you do this to me?"

"Because I didn't know what else to do. You told me something in confidence, and I'm trying to keep my word to you while at the same time I'm trying to be fair to your mother. Besides, a week ago, you told me you were questioning your sexuality, now you're a confirmed lesbian ready to jump in the sack. It doesn't matter if you're seventeen or twenty-seven, my advice is the same: Take some time and really think about what you're doing. I'm gonna tell you a story."

Harper shoved both hands into her hair. "This family and their stories."

Noel ignored her and continued. "I was eighteen, and I was dating a girl who'd just come out. I was crazy about her, and I thought she felt the same about me. For six months, it was all sex and good times, then one day outta the blue, she dumped me. She told me she thought she was gay but realized she wasn't." Noel snapped her fingers. "Just like that, she was done with me. It was devastating. I felt unwanted, especially sexually, and that messed with me for a long time. Has it occurred to you that after being intimate with Lydia, your feelings may change about her?"

Harper shook her head as she stared out the windshield. "For the first time in my life, I feel completely normal. I kept thinking a guy would come along, and I'd melt like Corey does every other day. I really didn't understand why my heart never raced when I looked at even the hottest ones. Lydia can just brush up against me accidentally, and I get all shaky. It did happen fast...just like magic. She's so sweet, and she makes me feel beautiful. Every second I spend with her makes everything I feel grow stronger."

Noel leaned her head against the back of her seat. "I understand. That's how I feel about Sunny, and it happened fast for me, too. That's why I'm not the person who needs to help you stay grounded because I'm floating, too."

Harper narrowed her eyes as she turned to Noel. "You just couldn't stay away from her, even though I asked you to. And you've already had sex!"

"I just basically told you that I'm not a good role model!" Noel blew out a sigh. "She's not like the others, Harpy. I'm not myself, which is a good thing, I guess. What I feel for her scares me. It's already so intense, and I keep telling myself to slow down, but I can't."

"Wow," Harper said, dragging the word out. "You're as fucked up as I am."

"Harper!"

Harper looked just like Inez when she sucked her teeth. "It's just a word. I didn't stomp a puppy." She breathed out heavily. "Tell me why you're scared, and I'll tell you what scares me."

Noel put a hand over her heart. "This feels so wonderful. I'm afraid it's all a dream that will end."

"What if when Lydia sees me naked, she won't want me anymore?"

"Oh, Harpy," Noel said sadly. "We all have things about our bodies we wish we could change." She reached out and laid a hand on Harper's shoulder. "If Lydia really loves you, she'll adore every inch of your body because it's yours."

"This is why I don't talk to Mom about things like this. She never admits that anything scares her, but I know everything does. She's too busy trying to make me feel like she's got it all under control. It's actually kind of comforting to me to hear you say you're just as messed up as I am."

"I'm sure she's trying to make you feel secure, so you can just enjoy this time of your life when things are supposed to be simple. They're anything but, though. Here's an ugly truth, it doesn't get any easier. That's why I want you to take your time with this. Ethan was right when he said this is the time to savor every moment because first love is the sweetest."

"The girl you told me about, was she your first love?"

"I thought she was," Noel said honestly. "Then there was a string of what I thought were loves, too. Come on, let's go inside."

"Why didn't you just take me home?"

"Because your mom would want to know why you're back. I'm still trying to give you the opportunity to tell her what's going on in your own time, but I hope you make that decision soon because you're about to give me a stroke." Noel climbed out of the car. "Move fast, your grandmother might be outside throwing something at animals."

Chapter 19

Noel was asleep at her desk during her lunch break when the receptionist's voice came over the speaker on her phone. "Dr. Savino, your mother is on line one."

"Of course she is. Her internal sensor went off indicating I had one moment's peace." Noel picked up the handset. "Hey, Mom."

"The shit is all over the fan, and you're at work! Harper told Mary that she's gay and in love with Lydia. Mary stayed home because she's all upset. Your father went fishing, so he can have fish to wrap in newspaper to lay on anyone's doorstep that messes with his baby. He's going all Godfather. You knew about this, Noel. Don't lie to me, you knew."

"Harper confided in me, but she wanted to be able to tell y'all when she was ready, and obviously, she's ready." Noel looked at her watch. "I'll talk to Mary when I get home, but right now, I have to get back to work."

"Yeah, well, just step over the fish wrapped in newspaper when you go into your house."

Noel walked into a circus when she entered her parents' home that evening. "Your father stole a gay flag!" Inez squawked.

"For the millionth time, Inez, I didn't steal it! The whole thing, pole and all, was lying on the ground beside a ditch, so I picked it up." Joe shrugged. "I thought it'd be a nice gesture," he said with his voice rising on every word. "I'm showing my support here! They don't exactly sell gay teddy bears at the bait store, and I've been seeing that flag for weeks on the ground."

Harper sat at the kitchen table beside her mother, her chin in her hand. She and Mary looked as though they had been crying. Noel went to Mary first and kissed the top of her head, then moved to Harper and gave her a hug.

"I'm glad you're here now, sit down," Mary said firmly. Noel's butt had not even reached the wood when Mary went off on her. "You knew, and you didn't say anything! I gave her permission to sleep at that girl's house last night based on—"

"Momma, I told you I didn't stay there."

Mary's stare was fixed on Noel. "Anything could've happened! And while I'm grateful that you intervened, you should have told me then. *I* am her mother, not you. I think what the real problem here is that Harper sees you as a role model, and maybe that's my fault for allowing her to spend as much time with you as she does. I also think that her love for you has clouded her judgment, and she's emulating you."

"I know who and what I am," Harper said emphatically.

"No, Harper, I don't think you do. You're surrounded by your aunt, your lesbian friend, her mother, her uncle, this whole gay culture. What you need right now is to step back and clear your head."

Harper stared at her in horror. "What does that mean?"

Mary put both hands on the table. "I have spent the day trying to reason with you, but you're not hearing me, so you're gonna take a break from seeing Lydia for a while, and—"

Harper sprang to her feet. "You're punishing me for being honest? I can't fucking believe this."

"Watch your mouth," Mary and Inez snapped at the same time.

Harper's voice trembled as she said, "The second I turn eighteen, I'm gone." She pushed past Inez when she reached for her and ran out the back door.

Joe made a move to follow, but Mary held up a hand. "Let her go. She can cool down while I talk to Noel."

Inez put a hand on Mary's shoulder. "Baby, let's all just take a moment to cool down."

"I'm as calm as I'm going to get, Momma. Harper is my child." Mary slammed her fist on the table and glared at Noel. "You better than anyone know how hard it is to lead the life you do. You should've been trying to talk her outta this instead of goading her into it. I thought you loved her more than to let her be someone who gets beaten up for being gay or hear someone brand her as depraved. She can't even get married in her own state! If there's even the slightest chance that she's not gay, I want her to find it. So back off, Noel."

"And after she's finished soul searching and she still is, then what?" Noel asked as calmly as she could.

Mary shook her head. "She's not gay, she's not. I'm not letting her go down this road."

Noel stared at her completely stunned. "Are you serious? Do you honestly think she would choose this? Do you think I did?"

"I want my child to be happy, not jumping from one person to another for cheap thrills."

"I am happy, damn it!" Noel slapped the table. "How happy are you, Ms. Straight and Narrow-minded? Your Prince Charming is in prison, your castle repossessed!"

"Stop! Just stop this right now," Inez said and sat down. "Heated blood is doing the talking here. Let's take a minute to breathe."

Mary stood abruptly. "We could've talked before, but Noel blew her chance with me, and now she needs to stay away from me and my daughter until I can get this all sorted out."

"That's just really fucked up," Noel said, shaking her head. "Next time Mom says the family oath, don't raise your glass because it'll make you a liar, you narrow-minded jackass. Go back to your house and try to brainwash your daughter. Maybe I'll feel sorry for you one day when she has nothing to do with you."

"Noel, shut your mouth," Joe ordered. He pointed to the chair that Mary had vacated. "Sit down."

"I'm sorry, Dad, but no, I'm done," Mary said.

"I said sit down," Joe bellowed, then cleared his throat when Mary complied. "Nobody makes parting shots around here but me and your mother. This family works things out, it's what we do. There's some underlying stuff going on here," he said as he swirled a finger. "It gets settled today. No one leaves this table until it does." He pulled out a chair and sat down. "Noel, apologize to your sister."

Noel's eyes flashed open wide. "For what?"

"The comment about the castle was totally outta line." Joe motioned at her. "Say you're sorry."

"I'm not."

"Ruth Noel!"

Noel jutted her bottom jaw out so far she looked like a bulldog and refused to look at Mary. "I am…sorry that what I said came across as mean, but what I meant was that even though you're straight, your life hasn't been a picnic, either."

Joe waved a hand. "Now apologize for calling her a liar."

"I can't," Noel said calmly. "I feel I've been lied to when she led me to believe that she didn't have a problem with me being gay."

Joe looked at Mary expectantly. She sat back and licked her lips. "I don't. I have a problem with Harper being gay."

"Same thing!"

"No, it's not!"

"What? I gotta put bibs on you two for this? One of you surprise me, step up, and be an adult here." Joe frowned at Inez as she got up. "Where're you going?"

"To make popcorn."

He stabbed a finger at her chair. "Sit."

Mary folded her arms and sighed. "Harper's changed over the last few weeks, and that occurred right about the time she and Lydia started hanging around together. She's been short with me, she seems very distracted, and when I try to talk to her, she just claims she's tired. And now, all of the sudden, she's gay. I can't help but think this has been brought on by peer pressure."

"Baby, we've talked about this before, years ago even, when all she could talk about was that teacher, Mrs. Seymour. We wondered then if she was gay because Noel did the same thing."

"That's right, and you told me then not to worry because kids go through phases," Mary said emphatically. "I was rolling with that."

Inez sucked her teeth and shook her head. "I think this is more than a phase. Noel, weigh in."

"I think her feelings for Lydia are genuine."

Mary closed her eyes and sighed. "This isn't what I wanted for her. I was mad earlier when I said those things, but I meant them. I don't know how y'all handled it with Noel. I turn on the news, and I hear people using words like depravity and comparing gay marriage to bestiality, and it incenses me. It's hard enough to deal with when it comes to my sister, but my daughter? I'd be sitting in prison just like David if someone made the mistake of uttering those things in front of me."

"As horrible as that is, you can't expect Harper not to be who she is just because you want to protect her," Inez said as she gazed at Noel. "I had to accept that long ago when times were different."

"You used to go to church all the time," Mary said and looked at her parents. "We all did. That stopped when Noel came out, and we never discussed it. How do you reconcile this with what we all grew up hearing?"

Inez massaged her temple while she thought for a moment. "I used to be caught up in all the dogma, content to have someone else tell me who God is and how I should act. I said my prayers, went to confession, made sure you kids learned and respected all that I knew. But when I found out about Noel, I began to question everything, and I wasn't finding any answers. Noel wasn't like you, even as a baby. She wanted trucks and dirt and Matt's clothes. She was too little to consider sexuality, she just wanted to play with the things that interested her. It was her nature." Inez shrugged. "Lots of girls are tomboys, they grow out of it, but Noel, she never did. Your father and I raised all of you kids the same way, and still she turned out to be different. She didn't choose it, it chose her. So I had to ask myself, if she wasn't meant to be, then why is she? And how could that be fair to a human being? That's when I began to really talk to God, like I'm doing with y'all now, and God talks to me."

"And what do you hear?" Noel asked.

"I hear, be nicer to Joe, but I'm pretty sure that's Charlotte, his mother, because she was always a buttinsky," Inez said seriously. "God talks to me in ways I understand, not in that crazy build-a-compound-because-you're-the-chosen-one sorta way, but through my kids and my grandkids. If before you were born, I sat down and wrote a book that I felt held absolutely everything you should know, do you think I'd say 'refer to the manual' when you asked me a question? Or would I put it in the hands of someone else who would more than likely add their own opinions?" Inez jerked a thumb at her chest. "I'd want my babies to talk to me for the relationship and because I tell y'all the truth."

"I struggle with that," Mary admitted. "I always have."

"Why didn't you say anything?" Joe asked.

Mary shrugged. "I guess I thought y'all had turned your backs on religion."

"We did, but not on God." Joe held up a hand. "We love unconditionally, and we leave practices and traditions to those who put their faith in them."

Noel rubbed the back of her neck. "I've had my struggles with it, too. I understand where you're at, Mary."

"I'm sorry that my concerns make me look like a homophobe," Mary said as she met Noel's gaze. "I've had blinders on when it came to Harper. I had suspicions, but when she confirmed them, all my fears…my insecurities came flying out. I…will work my way through this, but it's not gonna happen overnight."

Noel nodded and scrubbed at her face. Her voice broke when she said, "Please don't keep her from me."

At the first sign of tears, Joe retreated. "I have to go to the bathroom," he said quickly as he jumped up.

Mary swallowed hard. "That was the anger talking when I said that." She reached over and took Noel's hand. "I need you to help me through this…and Harper, too."

"I'm sorry, but I can't try to convince her to ignore her nature."

"I know. I can't, either. What I'm saying is that while I come to terms with this, I need you to be there for both of us."

Noel nodded. "I can do that."

Joe walked back into the room. "Um...Noel, where's your car?"

Chapter 20

When Sunny arrived that evening, a thrill shot through her when she spotted Noel's car in her driveway. She was exhausted from lack of sleep the night before and the long day she'd just endured, but she suddenly felt supercharged as she jogged toward the house. "Where's Noel?" she asked excitedly when Ethan opened the back door.

"She's not here," he whispered. "There's drama afoot."

Sunny's face fell. "What happened?"

"Harper showed up a couple of hours ago completely hysterical. She came out to her mother this morning, and they spent the day arguing. The mother thinks that Harper is being negatively influenced by us and Noel, so she's forbidden Harper to see us. So naturally, Harper stole Noel's car and came here. They're in Lydia's room talking privately, and I have a crick in my neck from hiding in the linen closet."

Ethan paused for a moment and listened before continuing softly. "I heard Harper tell Lydia that while she was standing outside trying to get herself together, she heard her mother and Noel screaming at each other. They must still be going at it because no one has shown up here for Harper."

"I really didn't expect this kind of reaction out of Mary." Sunny pulled her phone from her jacket and looked at it. "I don't have any missed calls or texts from Noel."

"Sunny, they're talking about running away if Mary sticks by what she says. I disconnected the battery cables in Lydia's truck," Ethan whispered. "I would've taken the whole battery if I'd had two hands."

Sunny was trying to process everything Ethan had just dropped on her when Lydia and Harper walked into the kitchen hand in hand. "Mom, we need to talk," Lydia announced.

Harper's eyes went wide as she looked at something over Sunny's shoulder. "Oh, shit."

Sunny whirled around, and Noel's angry face was pressed into one of the windowpanes. As she opened the door, Noel rushed in. "You are a master of making a tense situation a complete disaster!" Noel said angrily. "What were you thinking?"

"I know you're mad, but I had to see Lydia. Mom took my phone today, I couldn't even call her."

Noel pointed at the door. "She's waiting for you, go."

"No, I'm never going back," Harper said resolutely.

"Listen to me very carefully," Noel said as she clasped her hands together so tightly the tips of her fingers turned white. "Your mom has had time to get her thoughts together. Harper, go get in that car, and have a reasonable conversation with her, so the two of you can work this out."

Harper chewed her lip and stared at Noel as she debated. She exhaled heavily and turned to Lydia. "I'll be back, I promise." She kissed Lydia quickly and gave Noel a wide berth as she walked to the back door.

"My keys." Noel held out her hand. Harper pulled them out of her pocket and tossed them to her before closing the door.

Ethan cleared his throat. "Noel, can I make you something to drink?"

"No, thank you. I apologize for all the drama tonight." She gazed at Sunny and noticed that she was still wearing her jacket. "Did you just get home?"

"Uh-huh."

"Could we all sit down and talk for a minute?" Noel asked.

Sunny motioned to the kitchen table. "Please."

Noel took a deep breath and tried to calm down. "I really am sorry that you were hit with this as soon as you walked in." She pulled out a chair for Sunny. She patted Lydia on the shoulder. "Everything is gonna be okay."

When everyone was seated, Noel scrubbed at her face. "I'm so embarrassed that I came in here like a raging bull."

"It's okay, stop apologizing." Sunny took her hand. "Tell us what's going on."

Noel recounted the conversation she'd had with Mary and smiled at Lydia. "My sister doesn't dislike you. My whole family thinks you're great, myself included. Harper's gonna be grounded for a week because she took my car. I tried to plead her case, but I was overruled. After she serves her sentence, you'll be able to see her again."

"Are you sure?" Lydia asked nervously.

"Unless she does something else nutty, but otherwise, yes," Noel assured.

"Thank you." Lydia still looked disappointed about not being able to see Harper for a week.

Sunny patted her on the shoulder. "Why don't you go shower?"

Lydia nodded and got up, and after she walked out of the room, Ethan whispered, "I'll go outside and put her truck back together. There's a pot of soup on the stove."

Sunny gazed at Noel. "You look like you've been through the wringer. Would you like something to eat?"

"I should go and let you get some rest."

"Eat with me, and let's have a glass of wine. You look like you need it." Sunny stood and kissed Noel. "I'm just happy that I get to see you tonight."

Noel rested her head against Sunny's stomach and wrapped her arms around her waist. "Just let me hold you for a second. Wow, you've got lions fighting in there."

Sunny ran her hands through Noel's hair. "The plant caters the meetings, but I was so busy I never got a chance to eat."

Noel released her and got up. "Then let me serve you. Where are the bowls?"

Sunny took her by the hand and led her to the stove. "You open the wine," she said as she removed the lid on the soup. "It's vegetable, so I think red would work."

Noel selected a bottle from the rack on the cabinet and took the corkscrew Sunny handed her. "I have a feeling that a few sips of this will knock me on my ass. I was dragging at the office today. I even skipped lunch and tried to nap, but Mom called and messed that up."

Sunny filled one of the bowls and set it aside and picked up the other one. "Stay with me tonight."

Noel looked up from the bottle she was opening. "All night?"

"Yes, I'll get you up early enough to go home and get dressed in the morning. I want to cuddle up next to you and sleep."

"I'd like that," Noel said with a smile.

They took their dinner and the wine to the table and sat down. "I want to tell you that I don't think less of Mary for how she reacted. She's human and entitled to her own emotions. At least when she calmed down, she was willing to be open-minded. That never happened with my parents. It was convert or be exiled."

"Thank you for being so understanding." Noel shook her head as she thought. "She's just afraid for Harper. I am, too. I know what I've faced, I don't want anyone to be cruel to her."

"We can't stop that. Regardless of sexuality, people are always going to find a way to degrade another human being. Our job is to stand with our kids and teach them self-respect."

Ethan walked in and went straight to the sink where he washed his hands. "The battery is hooked back up," he whispered.

"Was something wrong with it?" Noel asked.

"Our girls were considering running away," Sunny said calmly. "Ethan unhooked Lydia's battery."

"I would've done yours, too, but Harper locked your car. I'm just thankful it didn't come down to me spiking your tires."

"Me too," Noel said distractedly. "Harper has lost her mind."

"Yeah, they're a little crazy right now. We're going to have to keep an eye on them." Sunny stroked the concern out of Noel's face. "They'll settle down when they feel they have our support."

"She gets like this during stressful situations," Ethan said and pointed at Sunny. "This eerie calm comes over her, and she's all laid back when I'm running around screaming. It's disconcerting and comforting at the same time. Sometimes, she even laughs."

"Except for haunted hayrides," Sunny conceded.

Sunny sighed as she listened to the water turn on in her bathroom. She would've loved to jump into the shower with Noel, but instead, she went into Lydia's room. She found Lydia sitting crossed-legged at the foot of her bed. "You okay?"

"I am now after talking to Noel. I'm bummed about Harper being grounded, though."

"It's only a week," Sunny said as she rubbed Lydia's shoulder. "Let me tuck you in like I used to."

Lydia grinned. "You are so goofy."

"I can't help it when it comes to you." Sunny turned the covers back and waited for Lydia to climb in. She pulled them up to her chin, then sat beside her and stroked her hair. "I'm your most ardent supporter, you know that, right?"

Lydia nodded and held her gaze.

"If there's a problem, we can always solve it together."

"I know Ethan was eavesdropping on me and Harper tonight, I could hear him bumping around in the closet. This is about Harper saying she wanted to run away, isn't it?"

"Would you really consider that?"

Lydia's reply was prompt. "No. That's what I wanted to talk to you about when we came into the kitchen. I was going to ask if she could stay with us. I know you've got my back."

Sunny smiled. "That's right, I do. If Harper's situation was bad, if she was being abused or neglected, I'd take her in with open arms. Her family isn't like that, though. She was upset and angry and made some rash decisions. I'm glad you kept your head and that you wanted to come to me to work out a solution, promise you always will."

"I do," Lydia said with a nod. "Is Noel staying here tonight?"

Sunny nodded with a look of concern. "Does that bother you?"

"No, it makes me happy," Lydia said with a smile. "I'm jealous, but I'm happy. Is it getting serious?"

"Yes, it is," Sunny said with a smile.

"I'm glad it's her. I really like Noel. She scared the crap out of me when I saw her face in the window tonight, but I think she's cool."

Sunny laughed softly as she kissed Lydia's forehead. "I like Harper, too. She's sweet, and I think you make an adorable couple."

"Me too," Lydia said proudly. "You and Noel aren't bad to look at, either, unless you're kissing."

Sunny kissed Lydia again and poked her in the chest. "I love you."

"Love you, too, and no fooling around. It's a work night, you go to sleep."

"Yes, ma'am." Sunny got up and switched off the light. When she went into her own room, Noel was already in bed. "Oh, you look cozy."

"I am, and let me say that as a dentist, I think the fact you have half a dozen new toothbrushes on hand is freaking awesome."

"Ethan orders them in bulk online. I'm sure you probably saw the mountain of floss I have, too."

"Yes! It turned me on."

"You're so kinky." Sunny took the remote from in front of the TV and handed it to Noel. "I'll be quick, don't fall asleep without me."

She bathed as fast as she could and went through her nightly routine of moisturizing and taking care of her teeth, which she knew was going to become an even bigger deal with Noel around. But if her sexy dentist wanted to give her flossing lessons, Sunny decided she'd be a willing student. Wrapped in her robe, she returned to the bedroom where Noel was transfixed by whatever she was watching.

"Look, this is a botched boob job, one is them is shaped like a fat banana because the implant detached. They're gonna..."

Noel fell silent when Sunny took off her robe. "Yours are perfect, by the way."

"Is it possible for us to sleep together naked without having sex?" Sunny climbed into bed and gazed at Noel.

"As tired as I am, I still want to, but I am thrilled at the prospect of just holding you close all night." Noel switched the TV off. "Do you want to be spooned or would you like to lie with your head on my shoulder?"

Sunny pecked Noel on the lips. "Spoon."

"Roll on your side and switch off the light."

Sunny did and groaned when Noel moved in close behind her and wrapped an arm around her waist. "I'm so glad you stayed," she said with a sigh.

"This is going to ruin me, you know." Noel yawned and kissed Sunny's shoulder. "I wish you the sweetest of dreams."

"I think I'm having one right now."

Noel settled and became very still. The warmth of her body and the feeling of being held soothed Sunny inside and out. She smiled thinking that she'd been ruined, too.

Sunny awoke the next morning before her alarm went off. Noel was on her stomach, and she was lying halfway on top of her. She had vague recollections of turning over during the night, and Noel rubbing her back and shoulders until she drifted off again. Not since Tamara had she felt so content. She wanted to spoil Noel rotten and keep her coming back every night. Gently, she moved away from the warm body beneath hers and climbed out of bed. With her robe on, she went into the kitchen and made a pot of coffee.

When Sunny returned to the bedroom, Noel was in the same position. She set the coffees on the bed stand and climbed in next to her, showering her shoulders and back with kisses. "I brought you coffee in bed," she whispered against Noel's skin when she began to stir. "I'll do it again tomorrow morning."

"Then I'll be back tonight," Noel said sleepily.

"That's exactly what I wanted to hear. Did you sleep well?"

"I feel like we just turned off the light. I was down deep."

"You don't remember petting on me, rubbing my shoulders?"

Noel lifted her head off the pillow. "No," she said, sounding surprised.

"You did, every time I turned over."

"Was it annoying?"

"No, I loved it. Are you ready for me to turn on the light?"

Noel flopped back down. "Yes," she said with dread. "I'll drag you back down and make you late for work if you don't."

Sunny switched on the lamp. "Two creams, two sugars, right? That's what you put in your coffee the first day you came to the house."

"You pay attention." Noel sat up, leaned against the headboard, and pointed to her mouth. "I'd kiss you good morning, but it's all bad in here."

"Aw, look at your sleepy little face," Sunny said as she handed Noel a cup. "Your eyes are all puffy, your hair is messy, you're adorable."

Noel grinned. "You think I'm cute."

"Yeah, I do." Sunny scooted up next to Noel shoulder to shoulder and picked up her own cup. "Tell me what a typical day is like."

"Well, I go in and check email, then I look at my schedule. By eight, my first patient is in the chair, and I hop until lunch. I usually eat at the office, but sometimes, Will and I go out. After lunch, I see patients until we close. That's about it for me. What's yours like?"

"I check my mail like you do, then I search for any accident reports that may've been submitted during the night. If it's really bad, like significant damage or someone was injured badly enough to warrant a hospital trip, they usually call me then. Most of what I do is assessments to determine what caused the incident. Almost every single one is because someone didn't follow protocols. I submit my findings to the supervisor of that department, and they handle reprimands. The other part of my job is going through procedures for every division of the plant and making sure they're up to date. In other words, I mostly sit in front of a computer."

"Are there a lot of incidents?"

"Every single day, but they're mostly minor, which is really saying something because the plant is huge."

Noel grinned before she sipped her coffee. "Do you wear a little hard hat?"

"I do when I'm out in the plant."

Noel's brow shot up. "Really?"

Sunny nodded. "And fire retardant coveralls."

"Sexy," Noel said with a growl. "I'm so serious. Take a picture of yourself dressed like that today and send it to me."

"I will if you send me one of you in the cat ears."

"Well, it's Wednesday, so that's bumblebee day, but I'll make an exception for you."

Sunny laughed. "Send me both."

Chapter 21

Lydia didn't know if Harper's grounding meant she couldn't ride to school with her or not, and Harper hadn't responded to her texts, so she showed up in front of the house at the regular time. Her heart sank when there was no sign of Harper, but Mary stepped outside of the Savinos' house and walked briskly toward her truck. Lydia rolled the window down and stiffened, unsure of what to expect.

"Good morning, Ms. Guidry."

"Hey, sweetie," Mary said with a smile. "Look, Harper is grounded for taking Noel's car without permission. She won't be able to ride with you until Monday."

"I understand," Lydia said glumly.

"There's something else I want to talk to you about. I know that Harper told you about our conversations, but I want you to know that I have nothing against you. Harper and I are doing a lot of talking, and we're trying to understand each other. There will be rules that she has to follow while dating you. I'd expect her to follow the same if she were dating a boy."

"Yes, ma'am, I'll respect them, too."

Mary smiled. "Thank you. I'm sure Noel will do this, too, but I want to invite you to dinner Sunday, you and your mom. I hope you'll come."

Lydia nodded. "I'll be there."

"Great, I hope you have a good day at school."

"You too—at work, I mean. Bye."

Mary waved and started back toward the house as Lydia drove away.

At lunch, Harper met Lydia in the courtyard and threw her arms around her heedless of anyone who might've been paying them any attention. "I know Mom told you I was grounded," Harper said as she released her.

"Yeah, but she didn't try to kill me, and she invited me to dinner Sunday."

"We've been talking a lot." Harper shrugged. "It's been kinda nice. I miss you, though. It's killing me not to be able to at least text you."

"I know. It was so strange not talking to you before I went to sleep. Your mom mentioned dating rules, what are they?"

Harper clamped her lips together tightly before saying, "I can't spend the night anymore, then it's just the typical stuff, midnight curfew, no sex blah blah. But now you can come to my house and hang out…when she's there, of course."

"Let me ask you out on an official date then. Will you go to the movies with me next Friday night?"

Harper shrugged. "Depends on what we're gonna see."

"The only answer I want to hear from you is yes," Lydia said with a smile.

"My answer to you will always be yes."

"Horny monkey, look at that," Noel whispered as she gazed at the photo that Sunny sent her decked out in a hard hat, coveralls, and boots. "Hey, this is my girlfriend." She held her phone up to Courtney when she walked by her in the break room.

"Why does she look familiar?"

"Because she came in here not too long ago with her uncle. He had the fishbone stuck in his gum."

Courtney grinned. "I thought I sensed something going on there. You were flirting, and I think she was, too." She pulled her lunch from the fridge, began to open it, and stopped. "I've worked with you going on three years, and this is the first time you have ever shown me a picture of someone you were dating."

"This one is special," Noel said as she continued to stare at the photo.

"So when's the wedding?" Courtney quipped.

"Spring, I think."

Sunny snatched her phone up when it vibrated on her desk and opened the attachments Noel sent her. She covered her mouth with her hand and chuckled at a photo of Noel wearing the cat ears and a goofy smile. Then she played the video Noel sent. At first, there was nothing but an empty hallway, then Noel suddenly appeared lying across a stool as it rolled, her arms outstretched as though she were flying with two black and yellow bee antennae on her head.

Sunny cackled. "She's insane and so adorable."

She watched the video repeatedly, wishing the day would move faster just so she could go home and be with Noel. It was a euphoric feeling to be so enamored and know that Noel felt the same. Sunny felt that they were beginning a journey together that she hoped would last a lifetime. Part of her already believed it would. She was no longer taking tentative steps, she was all in.

At the last bell, Harper raced to her locker in hopes of spending a few minutes with Lydia in the parking lot before she had to ride home with Corey and Mason. Corey appeared just as Harper put in her combination on the lock. "Aunt Mary texted me and said to tell you to meet her at the carpool line."

"What?" Harper said as her heart sank. As Corey began to repeat what she'd just said, Harper stopped her. "I heard you, I was just surprised."

"You want me to give your girlfriend a message if I see her?" Corey asked with a smirk.

A caustic retort was on the tip of Harper's tongue, instead she said, "Tell her I love her."

Pure satisfaction spread over Corey's face. "I knew that all along. It's totally cool. She's a little cutie."

Harper could never be sure if her cousin was being genuine or not, she used the same snide sounding tone for just about every conversation. "Thanks."

"See you in the morning," Corey said as she walked off.

Harper headed to the carpool line wondering why her mother had taken off work early, and more importantly, why she was there. When she spotted the car, Mary was waving at her with a smile. Harper tossed her book sack into the backseat and climbed into the front.

"Were you afraid that I might try to ride home with Lydia?"

"No." Mary looked surprised and a little disappointed by the question. "It's a beautiful day, and Vincent let me knock off early. I thought we might go to that yogurt place with all the do-it-yourself toppings. We haven't been there in a while."

"Oh, okay," Harper said with a nod.

"Were you considering riding with Lydia?"

"No, I don't want to be grounded longer. Corey would rat me out in a heartbeat."

Mary sighed. "That's an honest answer, though I would've preferred to hear you say you respect my rules."

"I always have."

"Until recently."

"I took Noel's car in an act of desperation. All I heard was that I wasn't going to be able to see Lydia again. I freaked, my bad, I'm sorry. I'd just like to put it out there for the record that I have never pulled a Corey and been caught sneaking outta the house or having sex in my bedroom. Oh, and I've never stolen the cash outta your purse."

"I agree, you've always been a good kid."

"I'm on the honor roll, too."

Mary nodded. "I'm very proud of that."

"I've never been drunk and given my underwear away."

Mary's brow rose. "Corey did that, too?"

"Several times."

Mary shook her head. "I don't think I want you to tell me any more about her."

"She's a legend. One day, her statue will be right next to the badger in the courtyard. She'll be in her cheer uniform, a bottle of booze in one hand, her panties in the other."

"Oh, my God," Mary whispered as she drove slowly through the school parking lot.

"How was your day?"

"Really good, until I heard all that."

"What was the worst thing you ever did in high school?"

"I was a saint," Mary said with a smile.

"I'm past the age of believing that. You're always gonna be Mom in my eyes, but I'd kind of like to get to know the human."

Mary was quiet for a moment and finally said, "The big mascot they have painted on the side of the gym facing the parking lot used to be more than a giant badger head. When I was in school, it was a full body, and one night, some friends and I painted two big testicles on it. I really don't know why we did it, I guess we thought it would be funny…and it was."

Harper nodded. "I'll give you a point for creativity."

"I deserve more than that. I made one ball hang a little lower than the other for realism. If I had been graded on that art project, I'm certain I would've gotten an A."

"You know, I've seen your sketchbook that Nana keeps in that box with all the trophies and things. You were really good, why didn't you pursue that as a career?"

"Because there was something I wanted more. The most beautiful work of art I ever created was you."

Harper smiled. "That was sweet—corny, but sweet."

"It's true. I look back over my life, and you're the one thing that has always been perfect."

"Even now?"

"Always, Harper. I know I keep repeating myself, but it's important that you know that I don't see you or Noel or anyone else that is gay as gross, unnatural, or disgusting. What I struggle with is the stigma and the hate from those who do see you that way."

"Well, I'm fat, too, so they'll have plenty of ammunition."

"Just because you're not a size two doesn't mean you're fat. I hate to hear you say that."

"You're missing my point. People pick out something to hate on. It doesn't matter what I am, there's always going to be some prick that's gonna have something to say."

"They don't kill or beat people for being overweight," Mary argued.

"No, they kill them with words, and they suffer an emotional death."

Mary didn't have a rebuttal as she pulled into the lot of the yogurt shop and parked. She and Harper were both deep in their own thoughts as they loaded their frozen treats with toppings. After Mary paid for them, they went outside and chose a table in the sun.

"I think Lydia is very sweet, and I like that she's respectful."

"Are you just saying that to ease the tension?" Harper asked before taking a bite.

"Dear God, you have become my mother. She bites your face off with such a casualness you don't even know it's missing. I said what I meant," Mary snapped. "Can we just lower our defenses and talk?"

After a moment or two of silence, Harper said, "I'm glad you like her because she is very sweet." She took a bite of her yogurt and swallowed. "Lydia makes me feel beautiful. When she looks at me, all I see is love in her eyes. I know I can tell her anything that I'm thinking. Sometimes, she knows what I'm gonna say before I say it."

"That's a pretty intense bond for only knowing her a short time."

"I know, that's what makes it so special. I feel like I've always known her."

"She makes you feel weightless, like your feet aren't touching the ground. You see her face in a crowd, and your heart thunders in your chest. Everything is right with the world when she's by your side."

Harper gazed at Mary in wonder. "Yes, that's exactly what I feel."

Mary smiled wistfully. "It's magic."

"Did you feel that way about Dad?"

Mary nodded and looked away. "I did, and sometimes…all I can remember were those days."

"Are you afraid that I'll get hurt like you did?"

Mary nodded again. "But I pray you won't. Not every story has an unhappy ending." She slowly met Harper's gaze. "What happened was horrible, it broke me for a while. I know it sounds insane, but if I were given the chance to go back in time knowing that the end result would be the same...I'd do it all over, just to feel that magic again." Mary's eyes watered as she gazed at Harper. "So enjoy this, and we'll both hope that it lasts forever. If it doesn't, I'll be right by your side to help you back on your feet."

Chapter 22

Ethan threw open the door as Noel walked up with a pack slung over her shoulder. "Did Sunny tell you she was going to be late?"

"She did, but I wanted to be here when she gets home."

"Oh! Y'all are just so cute. Get in this house," Ethan said as he stepped out of the way.

Lydia dragged into the foyer with a disgusted look on her face. She was wearing an evening gown, her face heavily made up framed by a blond wig. "Go ahead, laugh, but please don't take any pictures or tell anyone you saw me like this, especially Harper."

Noel's face contorted as she tried to keep her laughter at bay. "Who are you?"

"Princess Grace Kelly!" Ethan exclaimed. "Isn't she beautiful?"

"Stunning is the word I'd use." Noel cleared her throat to cover a laugh as Lydia stared back at her glumly. "Stunning." She jumped when Ethan touched her cheek.

"Have you ever had a facial?"

"I moisturize." Noel stepped away. "A lot."

Ethan grabbed her by the arm and led her to the salon. "I'm going to take ten years off you in twenty minutes. You'll love it. I do Sunny's face all the time, and she doesn't look forty-one, does she?"

"No," Noel said nervously as he planted her in a chair.

Lydia staggered into the room, struggling to remain atop the high heels on her feet. "Can I take this off now?"

"No, I want Sunny to see you first." Ethan waved at her. "Take a seat, keep us company."

Lydia stumbled over to a chair and fell into it. "Sure, this can't get any more uncomfortable anyway."

Noel was certain that she looked as frightened as her young patients did the first time they sat in her chair. Ethan pulled her hair back and wrapped it in a towel. "You're pretty effective with that bad hand."

"I can do things like this. It's the cutting I have a problem with. Sunny has to help me when I do Lydia's hair, and Lydia steps in when I work on Sunny's. Now just relax, I'm going to recline your chair."

"Easier said than done, right?" Lydia asked as she sat with her legs apart and the dress falling between them.

Ethan shot her a look. "Sit like a lady."

"I put this dress on and let you do this to me. I should at least be allowed to be comfortable. I want to eat."

"Not in that dress you don't. The casserole will be ready soon." Ethan returned his attention to Noel and waved two oval pads. "I will cover your eyes with these to keep anything from getting into them. First, I will clean your face, next I will gently exfoliate, then I'll apply a mask that will make your skin smooth and supple." Ethan covered Noel's eyes and stared at her for a moment. "Oh, Noel," he said with a dramatic sigh. "With your facial structure, I could make you into Audrey Hepburn so very easily."

Sunny felt a thrill again as she turned into the driveway and spotted Noel's car. This time, she knew who waited inside for her. The idea of having dinner with Noel and relaxing for a while filled her with a sense of utter contentment. But when she began to think about what might happen later that night, the muscles in her stomach quivered. She raced to the back door and found the kitchen empty. She went into the living room next, and three women gazed back at her. Grace Kelly, Liz Taylor, and Audrey Hepburn stood in a row, their arms outstretched.

"Oh. My. God. Noel, honey, he got you, too."

"I'd walk over there and kiss you, but I don't think I'm gonna make it in these shoes." Noel smiled. "I've never worn an evening gown before, and tonight, I thought I might give it a whirl."

Noel was clad in a long black form-fitting gown. The wig was an updo piled atop her head. Black gloves went up to her elbows on both arms. Ethan had outdone himself on the understated makeup. She was gorgeous.

"You're lovely, all of you," Sunny breathed out on a sigh, but her gaze was set on Noel.

"Okay, she's seen us. Now can we take this stuff off?" Lydia asked impatiently.

"It seems so wrong to have gone to all that trouble just to look like that for a minute," Sunny said. "My vote is to leave it on during dinner."

Noel's and Lydia's faces fell while Ethan squealed with delight. He turned to Lydia. "You're going to have to use a towel for a bib because I don't want that dress stained."

"I'm a messy eater, I should change," Noel said.

"Oh, no, you're not. I've seen you eat, I'd almost describe the way you do it as dainty." Ethan gazed at Noel with a smile. "I trust you."

"Ladies," Sunny announced. "I will be serving dinner tonight." She walked over to Noel and held out her arm. "May I escort you?"

"Does that mean you're gonna carry me on your back? I wasn't joking when I said I can't walk in these shoes."

"I'll steady you while you slip them off your feet." Sunny watched as Ethan tried to teach Lydia the proper way to walk in heels as they made their way into the kitchen, then she gazed at Noel. "You are so damn hot," she whispered. "Is there anything you don't look delicious in?"

"I don't feel very tasty right now," Noel said as she kicked out of one of the heels.

"I'm totally turned on. I've got this whole butch thing going on inside, and I want to drag you into the bedroom and take you right now."

Noel arched one brilliantly sculpted eyebrow. "Seriously?"

"Leave the dress on, and I promise I'll take it off you as soon as Lydia goes to bed."

"That long?" Noel squeaked.

"It'll be worth the wait."

Noel kicked off the other shoe. "You've got a deal."

Sunny walked Noel to the table and pulled out her chair. Once she was seated, Sunny went to Ethan, who was placing salad into bowls. "Ms. Taylor, I'll take it from here."

"If you insist."

"I do." Sunny took him by the hand. She held it high as she walked him over to the table and seated him, as well.

Lydia poked at her own cleavage. "Now I know how people hide money and stuff in here." She grabbed a salt shaker and stuffed it between her breasts. "It's a little pocket."

"I'm so jealous," Ethan said. "Even with all my loose skin, I can only muster a B cup."

After dinner, Lydia dragged Ethan into the salon and made him remove all her makeup. Noel helped Sunny straighten up the kitchen. She covered what was left of the casserole as Sunny loaded the dishwasher, then leaned against the counter. "I feel like since I'm all dressed up, you owe me a dance."

Sunny closed the dishwasher and dimmed the lights overhead. "You'll have to teach me how to lead."

Noel smiled, took Sunny's hand, and led her to the French doors. "Wrap one arm around my waist, keep hold of my hand, and just sway with me."

Lydia and Ethan appeared in the doorway. "Aw, man, that's just gross," Lydia said with a laugh.

"Serenade us since we have no music," Sunny said as she dared to twirl Noel.

Ethan burst out with *Moon River* in a high falsetto.

"Dude, you're scaring the cat, she ran out of the room," Lydia said as she strode over to the dancing couple. "I'm calling it a night." She kissed Sunny on the cheek, and after a moment's hesitation, she did the same to Noel. "Y'all are dorks, I just want you to know that."

"One day, you'll be one, too," Noel called after her.

Ethan sighed happily. "Good night, ladies. You'll have to make your own music now."

Sunny slid her hand over Noel's backside. "Say the line."

"The rain in Spain makes the ground wet."

Sunny laughed and pressed her head to Noel's. "Have you ever seen *My Fair Lady*?"

"Yes, I have. I refuse to oblige your request. I'm not ready to give into this domination thing completely."

Sunny nuzzled her neck. "Relationships are give and take," she breathed against her skin. "And I want to take."

Noel's skin broke out in goose bumps. "I'll give you anything you want."

"For how long?"

"Forever," Noel said without hesitation. "My feet aren't touching the ground anymore, I know I'm falling."

"I'm going with you." Sunny brushed Noel's lips with her own. "I'm not afraid anymore."

Noel kissed her deeply and whispered, "Take me to your bedroom, make love with me for the first time."

Sunny's earlier intent to ravish Noel faded as she unzipped the back of the gown and let it fall to the floor. They covered each other in kisses and soft touches as clothing was stripped away. Noel sat on the bed and pulled Sunny with her. Soft light filled the room as Sunny stretched out over Noel, staring into her eyes, unafraid to let Noel see inside of her.

"You're beautiful," Sunny said. "And you're mine."

"Yes," Noel said as she pulled her down for a kiss.

Noel's touch was full of fire and affection as she ran her fingertips over Sunny's back. She wanted to remember every sensual second of the experience. She gladly accepted that her heart and her body were on the same page this time. Sunny's mouth on her skin filled her with arousal, and oddly, contentment because Noel felt she was finally, truly where she belonged.

Sunny entwined their fingers as she kissed her way to Noel's breasts, taking her time there, reveling in the feel of Noel's responses to each stroke of her tongue. She slipped lower, blazing a trail of kisses down Noel's stomach eager to please. This dance, Sunny knew well. She led Noel effortlessly through every step. The music was Noel's soft moans and the cadence of every breath, and the song ended much too quickly, but many more would play.

Chapter 23

"What are you wearing? You look ridiculous." Sunny said as she looked Ethan over.

He looked down at his men's trousers and gray dress shirt. "What's wrong with it?"

"It's not you."

"I want to make a good first impression," he said seriously.

"Then be you."

He jutted his chin. "I suppose my pink cardigan would go nicely."

"And some heels," Sunny called after him and went into her bedroom to check on Noel. She stood in the doorway of the bathroom and watched as Noel dried her hair. The vanity was full of Noel's things. More clothes seemed to fill the closet each night she came to what Sunny now considered their home, though they hadn't made it official.

When the hairdryer switched off, Noel did a double take at Sunny. "I thought you were Lydia. She's been in here three times urging me to hurry up."

"She's excited. Harper got her phone back today, and she told her that when dinner begins, her grounding is officially over."

Noel gazed at Sunny's navy blue sweater and jeans. "You look nice. You wanna step in here and close that door?"

"I do, but I'm pretty sure that Lydia would never forgive us." Sunny took Noel's shirt from the hanger hooked to the door and held it for her to slip into. "But tonight, I'll gladly take you up on that offer."

Lydia suddenly appeared in the doorway. "I'm gonna try and stuff Ethan in the car now since that takes time. Noel, can I have your keys?"

"They're on the dresser. We'll be right out." Noel grinned as Sunny buttoned her shirt and kissed her each time she closed one. She clasped Sunny's face in both hands when she finished and kissed her slowly. "Thank you for the best week of my life. I'm going to tell you that every Sunday from here on out."

"I love that you're big on tradition."

"What is the safety rating on this?" Ethan said as he stared at Noel's car.

"It's one of the best, it's got air bags everywhere, and Sunny will be driving," Noel said with a hand on his shoulder. "You can do this."

"Yes, I can." Ethan breathed out a sigh as he climbed in and put his seat belt on. Then he pulled his sleep mask down over his eyes. "I'm looking forward to meeting your family."

"Sweetie, that's probably the scariest thing you're gonna face all day. They wanna meet you, too, especially my mother. When she offers you a glass of wine, my advice is to take it," Noel said as she closed the door.

Noel climbed into the front passenger seat just in time to hear Lydia say, "Dude, don't be so jumpy."

"Hold my hand," Ethan said nervously. "What is that? Lydia, moisturize. Have I taught you nothing?"

Sunny got into the driver's seat and held out her hands. "I don't have to adjust anything."

"You're a perfect fit," Noel said and leaned over to kiss her before Lydia pitched a fit.

"Y'all have got to stop. You, like, kiss every five seconds. *Please*, make out later and take me to Harper."

"Do you think your father will like me?" Ethan asked nervously.

"Dad will think you're awesome," Noel assured.

"Oh, my God!" Ethan cried when Sunny started down the driveway.

Sunny hit the brakes hard. "We haven't even pulled onto the road yet."

"That's not it. I forgot the dessert!"

Lydia groaned with frustration. "It's in the trunk, probably plastered against the backseat now."

Ethan released a sigh. "You may continue on."

"What was that you made?" Noel asked.

"A fruit tart. I would've preferred fresh local berries, but you can't find them this time of year. I sent Lydia to the grocery store this morning, and she brought back things from Argentina. Oh, I hope they have flavor. You just don't know how long fruits and veggies are in transport before they reach the shelves."

Keep him talking, Sunny mouthed.

"What kind of berries?" Noel asked.

"Blackberries, raspberries, and blueberries. I think you're going to love it. I made the custard very sweet to offset the tanginess of the fruit. What was that?" Ethan demanded.

"Just a pothole," Noel said calmly. "She's driving very slowly, cars are stacked up for miles behind us. You should take that thing off your eyes so you can see the scenery. The fall leaves are very pretty." Sunny poked Noel and shook her head. "Or better yet, I'll just describe what I see and you can relax. Since this is one of the older neighborhoods in Baton Rouge, there are a lot of mature trees that're beautiful. A lot of the houses are wood framed, there are picket fences, and oh, there's a Great Dane, he's—"

"Oh, my God! Sunny, hit the brakes, those things are big as a horse!" Ethan screamed.

"He's behind a fence," Noel assured. "It's okay." Rattled from the outburst, she looked for something calming. "There are flowers and a cute little squirrel eating—"

"Don't hit it! It'll fly through the windshield and decapitate us all."

"It's a fake squirrel," Noel quickly amended.

"Ethan, tell us all about the time you stuck your doodle in the Silk Hands wax," Sunny said.

"What?" Lydia and Noel exclaimed at the same time.

"Sunny! I thought that was between us."

"I put my face in that one time, man! Gimme my hand back," Lydia said angrily.

"I switched out the wax immediately after. Don't you let go of me, Lydia."

Sunny sighed happily as she pulled to the curb in front of the Savino house. "I should've thought about that earlier."

Lydia jumped out of the car when Harper shot out of the front door. They met halfway and threw their arms around each other. "Now that is sweet," Ethan said as he pulled the mask from his eyes.

Noel opened the back door and extended her hand to him. "May I escort you?"

"I see why Sunny can't keep her hands off you, you're a charmer. And well, you filled out that dress the other night like nobody's business."

Sunny retrieved the tart from the trunk, and as they started up the front walk, Inez came out of the front door and shook a finger at Lydia and Harper. "You two, break it up or I'm gonna get the hose out."

"I'm just hugging her, Nana," Harper said, refusing to let Lydia go.

"Mom, this dashing young man is Ethan Chase," Noel said as Inez made her way to them.

Inez extended her hand. "I've been looking forward to meeting you."

Ethan took it gently and kissed it. "And you are more lovely than I imagined."

Inez grinned at Sunny. "I already love this guy."

Joe poked his head out the front door. "Inez, I took that cow outta the oven and sliced it. You must be Ethan," he said as he walked onto the porch. "I'm Joe, it's great to meet you."

"Likewise," Ethan said and shook his hand.

Joe moved to Sunny next and kissed her cheek as he took the tart from her. "You stole my daughter, she hasn't been home in days."

"Yes, sir, I did."

Joe shook his head as he gazed at her with a smile. "Not an ounce of guilt on that mug, either."

Sunny shrugged. "I can't even fake it."

"Get in that house. Hey, you lovebirds. Get in here, let's eat," he shouted to Harper and Lydia.

Ethan was introduced to the entire Savino family, then Inez latched on to him as everyone finished setting the table. She put a glass of wine in his hand and dragged him over to the window. "I know you cook, so I think you'll love this. Out there in that box covered with chicken wire is where I grow my herbs. I'm canning, too, you should see my storeroom, it's full of stuff. That's why Joe didn't do a garden this year because he says I've got too much."

"I would love to learn how to can my own foods. My neighbor is a gardener, and when we moved in over the summer, he brought over all kinds of vegetables." Ethan put a hand on Inez's arm. "Girl, I was in heaven."

Inez peered at him closely. "You got on mascara?"

"No, just a brush-on moisturizer, it keeps my lashes supple."

"I would kill for lashes like that."

"You should come over to the house one day. I'll give you a facial and an eyelash treatment."

"I wanna come," Lauren said and grinned goofily. "I shouldn't have invited myself, but I want to play, too."

Ethan threw up a hand and sang out, "Facial party."

"Aw, he has a play date with the Savino girls," Sunny whispered into Noel's ear.

"This is really scary. If he bonds with my mom…oh, my God."

"Can we eat now?" Joe bellowed from the living room.

"We eat when I say we eat!" Inez looked at the table to find it set to her satisfaction. "Now we eat."

The whole seating arrangement had been switched around to accommodate everyone. Instead of sitting at opposite ends of the table, Inez sat next to Joe, and Ethan sat on the other side of him. Matt sat at the other end with Lauren and their kids. Lydia and Harper sat side by side, and Mary was next to them. Noel and Sunny sat on the opposite side of the table.

Everyone quieted when Joe cleared his throat. "This is nice. Today, I'd like to break with tradition and say the blessing along with the family oath. Everybody okay with that?" he asked, looking at Inez specifically. After receiving her nod, Joe held out his hands to her and Ethan and bowed his head.

"Dear Lord, I thank you for my family, all of whom are seated at this table. Some of them don't know it yet, but I'm pretty sure they're stuck with us. Thank you for giving us the wisdom and the grace to always settle our disputes and be close as a family. Thank you for the good weather, and may the roast not be like shoe leather. And God, please bless Drew Brees. Amen."

They continued to hold hands as Joe stated his version of the oath. "At this table, we are all equal. Gay, straight, male, female makes no difference here because we are all one. What makes us different as a whole is that come what may, we will always stand united in love and mutual respect for one another because we are the Savinos. Now we eat."

Epilogue

Sunny awoke before dawn and reached for Noel, only to find her side of the bed empty. She'd tossed and turned the night before, unable to sleep without the warm body she'd gotten used to beside her. She got up and shrugged on her robe, shivering. It was early spring, but the house still held a chill. Only Tobi stirred as she stepped into the hall and buffed Sunny's legs as she made her way to the kitchen.

She set the coffee to brew and stared at her two favorite photos held to the refrigerator by magnets. The first was taken in downtown Baton Rouge at the theater where she and Noel and the girls saw *The Addams Family Musical*. They were huddled together in front of the marquee, their arms wrapped around one another. The next was taken on Broadway beneath a billboard bearing the face of the iconic green witch. Mary had snapped the picture as Sunny and Noel and the girls leapt into the air with tickets to *Wicked* clutched in their hands.

"What are you thinking at this very moment?"

Sunny turned to Ethan and smiled. "That I'm lucky...blessed."

Ethan frowned. "You look kind of terrified."

"Nervous, yes, afraid, no. I've never been more certain of anything. But do you know what I went to bed thinking about last night?"

"Your honeymoon, I'm sure."

Sunny shook her head. "Tamara."

"Oh, no." Ethan walked over and touched Sunny's face. "Don't do that now, not after all this time."

"I was just closing that chapter." Sunny smiled. "I am fine, I promise—would've been better with my fiancée, the stickler for tradition, by my side, but I'm great."

"The bride isn't supposed to see the bride before the commitment ceremony, which is a shame because she won't get the benefit of one of my facials."

"She's beautiful just the way she is."

Ethan sighed. "Spoken like a woman in love."

Noel walked to the back door of her house and threw it open. "Momma, what?"

"I bought one of those spanky things, and I can't get into it by myself."

"And that is a job for Mary." Noel stepped back and let Inez in. "What on earth are you doing with one of those anyway? You got the figure of a toothpick."

Ethan says it'll smooth out my hips and shape my ass under my dress. I guess I'll wait and squeeze into it when I get over there." She sucked her teeth. "Make coffee, what're waiting for? I can't stand around here all day, and neither can you. Noel, don't you go back to bed after I leave."

"There's no chance of me falling back to sleep now," Noel groused as she set up the coffeemaker. She opened the cabinet where she normally kept her cups and sighed. "Do you have any idea where Mary moved everything when she painted in here?"

"They're in a box in the dining room you always thought was a storeroom. This place is gonna be something when she's finished with it," Inez said as she admired the light yellow walls that really brightened the kitchen while Noel fished out the cups.

Noel only felt a slight twinge of anxiety as she looked at all of her things boxed up, but Mary was finally going to get to live in a house again. It made Noel happy that her sister was thrilled. The deal was that Mary would pick up the mortgage payments. If she ever decided to move out, Noel would sell the house and deduct what Mary had paid into it. Noel hoped, however, that Mary would always stay there.

Noel poured her mother a cup of coffee and set the machine to brew another. Inez pointed at it. "That's a piece of shit. You can get rid of it now, give it to Harper. She can use it in her dorm room this fall."

"I thought she was getting an apartment."

"Not until she finishes her freshman year in college." Inez turned as the back door opened. "Hey, we talk about y'all, and you show up. If you want coffee, you're gonna have to wait for it to brew one cup at a time."

Mary walked over to Noel and wrapped a simple silver bracelet around her wrist. "Something borrowed. I want this back."

Harper held up a box and opened the lid to reveal a royal blue silk handkerchief. "Something blue to go into the breast pocket of your vest."

"Aw, y'all are great," Noel said and kissed both of them. "Coffee?"

"No, thanks. Mom is gonna have to take hers to go. We should've already been at the other house by now," Mary said. "Ethan is doing our hair."

"I'll be behind y'all in a few. I wanna give Noel some advice," Harper said with a grin.

Inez kissed Noel and clamped a hand on her jaw. "Look me in the eye. You make sure your father is ready to leave the house at exactly twelve forty-five. This is not something you be late for."

Noel rolled her eyes. "Yes, ma'am."

"Fall in the fall, married by the spring. What did I tell you?" Inez said as Mary dragged her outside. "Your momma's brilliant. Don't forget that."

When the door closed behind them, Harper met Noel's gaze. "It's not exactly advice, it's a confession. I'm eighteen now. I'm an independent woman and—"

"You still live with your mother, shut up."

"As I was saying," Harper continued. "My confession is that I've been having sex in your old bed."

Noel bit her bottom lip. "You little nasty."

"A lot of sex. We park on the next block and sneak in here at night, so we won't be disturbed." Harper backed toward the door. "So just so you know, sex. Me and Lydia getting naked and freaky all up in your old bed." She clenched her fist and howled. "You can't say a thing because I'm eighteen and knocking boots. And let me tell you, I rock her world. That's right!"

Noel laughed. "Out, freak."

Noel tried not to fidget as she waited for the music to start. Ethan, Mary, Lauren, and her mother had done an outstanding job of transforming the yard into an outdoor wedding chapel. Instead of two rows on either side of the aisle, there was only one on the left signifying that they were all one family. She stood beneath an arch in the back beside her father clutching his arm tightly. Harper and Lydia were already standing in front with Joanna, an LGBT minister who would officiate the ceremony.

"They got the rings, right?" Joe asked nervously.

"Uh-huh."

Joe's gaze swept over the white sleeveless pantsuit Noel wore, the blue hankie protruding from her breast pocket. "You look beautiful, baby."

"Thank you, Dad."

"You look like a zombie, so don't trip and fall over that stupid runner thing we have to walk on."

"Uh-huh."

"If you start to feel pukish when you get up there…you're just screwed because there's nothing to hide behind. Go for your mother's purse, that thing is big enough to handle anything."

"Uh…huh."

"Your answers are not convincing me that you won't do a face plant on the way to the front."

"I don't like being the center of attention, especially in front of people I don't know. Where did they come from?"

"Well, you know Jeff, and those guys next to him are some fishing buddies. I felt rude for not inviting them. You know Greg and Rhonda, and I think your mother invited the woman from the post office because she's gay, too."

"I didn't even invite my friends, this was supposed to be a small family affair."

"It is, your family is all here." Joe straightened to his full height when the music began to play. "Come on. Don't make me drag you."

Noel didn't remember the walk down the aisle. She was barely cognizant of her father kissing her cheek and leaving her alone, when he went to sit with Inez. The only thing that grounded her as she waited for Sunny to make her walk was Harper, who leaned in close and whispered, "I will so get laid before you do."

Ethan and Sunny stood together just out of sight of the rear archway. Sunny gazed at Ethan in his cream-colored sheath dress and lavender satin sash. "You look spectacular."

"How's the wig? Is it too much?" he asked as a spindly brown curl fell across his face.

"No, brown is a good color on you."

Ethan gazed at Sunny's white pantsuit. "You are absolutely stunning, but I wish you would've worn a dress."

Sunny snorted. "People are gonna think you're the bride. You want to carry the flowers?"

"I would, but they're attracting bees."

Sunny squirmed. "My right butt cheek itches. I think something has already bitten me. You have nails, give me a scratch."

"I'm *not* scratching your butt. I would kill or die for you, but I am not…is that the third verse?"

"No, it's the third verse, we go on the third."

Ethan looked at her. "Did I not just say third?"

"Oh, shit."

The two of them dashed arm in arm into the archway, then tried to compose themselves while everyone stared back at them. Sunny clamped her lips together tightly and made a soft keening noise. Ethan squeezed her arm as someone restarted the music.

"Don't you dare laugh," Ethan murmured, trying not to move his lips.

Everybody in the audience thought that what they were seeing were tears of joy in Sunny's eyes. "Was that Danny DeVito in drag?" she mumbled and made the keening noise again. She glanced at Ethan when she heard him sniff. "Are you crying or laughing?"

"Both."

Sunny intentionally did not look at Noel until they were halfway down the aisle because she knew that she'd probably cry then, too, and she did. Ethan kissed her cheek and gave her hand to Noel. As they stood face to face, Noel smiled at her and whispered, "Thank you for the best day of my life."

Joe leaned close to Inez and whispered, "Did they write their own vows?"

"No, they went with the traditional stuff, shut up."

"Whew, I was afraid it was gonna be a long drawn out thing with poetry, I hate that. Are you crying?"

"No, that's Mary, she's blubbering like a fool."

Joe looked to his right and found Ethan sobbing. He pulled his handkerchief from his pocket and handed it to him. "Get it together old...gal," he said as he placed a hand on Ethan's shoulder.

"Sunny should've worn the sling-backs like I suggested, those shoes don't go with that outfit," Ethan sobbed. "But she looks so happy."

"Noel, do you take Sunny to be your partner in life, to have and to hold from this day forward, to love and honor, to cherish always, forsaking all others?"

Noel stared into Sunny's eyes dreamily, then jumped when Harper said, "Speak."

"Yes...I do...forever and ever and ever."

"Oh, my God," Harper whispered. "She's losing it."

Joanna smiled indulgently. "Sunny, do you take Noel to be your partner in life, to have and to hold from this day forward, to love and honor, to cherish always—"

"I do, I so do."

"Okay, just so we're clear, forsaking all others, right?" Noel asked.

"That was my line," Joanna whispered.

"Totally, absolutely," Sunny blurted out as she gazed at Noel. "You're the only one I want forever."

Joanna motioned to Harper for the ring. Noel's hands shook as she took it from her. "Repeat after me," Joanna said. "This ring is a symbol of my love for you, it has no end."

Noel licked her lips. "This ring…it has no end," she said as she slipped it onto Sunny's finger.

"I shoulda got her a hearing aid instead of a quilt for a wedding gift," Inez said as she covered her face with her hand.

Lydia handed Sunny Noel's ring and whispered, "Mom, don't jack this up."

"Repeat after me," Joanna stated once again. "This—"

"This ring is a symbol of my love for you, it has no end," Sunny said as she slipped it on Noel's finger.

Joanna nodded with a smile. "Okay, you two, you may kiss now."

"Whoa! That's how a Savino does it!" Joe exclaimed as he slapped Ethan on the back and nearly sent him out of his chair. "Now we eat!"

The makeshift dance floor was full of people doing the Electric Slide, but off by themselves, Noel and Sunny slowly swayed in each other's arms. "Thank you so much for not making me go out there, even though I got you a bowling ball for a wedding gift."

"That's okay, I bought us salsa lessons as my present to you."

Harper and Lydia walked out of the house. Harper's hair was messy, and Lydia's was wet. Harper winked as they quickly made their way back to the party. "Told ya," she called out with a grin.

"Do I want to know what that was all about?" Sunny asked.

Noel smiled and kissed her. "No, honey, I'm sure you don't."

"I love you," Sunny said with a happy sigh.

"I love you more."

"Not possible." Sunny grinned. "Is this our first argument?"

"One of many, I'm sure. I am a Savino after all, and now, you're one too."

About the Author

Robin Alexander is the author of the Goldie Award-winning *Gloria's Secret* and many other novels for Intaglio Publications—*Gloria's Inn, Gift of Time, The Taking of Eden, Love's Someday, Pitifully Ugly, Undeniable, A Devil in Disguise, Half to Death, Gloria's Legacy, A Kiss Doesn't Lie, The Secret of St. Claire, Magnetic, The Lure of White Oak Lake, The Summer of Our Discontent, Just Jorie, Scaredy Cat, The Magic of White Oak Lake* and *Always Alex*.

She was also a 2013 winner of the Alice B Readers Appreciation Award, which she considers a true feather in her cap.

Robin spends her days working with the staff of Intaglio and her nights with her own writings. She still manages to find time to spend with her partner, Becky, and their three dogs and four cats.

You can reach her at robinalex65@yahoo.com. You can visit her website at www.robinalexanderbooks.com and find her on Facebook.

Printed in Great Britain
by Amazon